The Unexpected Mail Order Bride

Hannah Winstone

Published by Trellis Publishing, 2021.

This is a work of fiction. Similarities to real people, places, or events are entirely coincidental.

THE UNEXPECTED MAIL ORDER BRIDE

First edition. July 4, 2021.

Copyright © 2021 Hannah Winstone.

ISBN: 979-8224419449

Written by Hannah Winstone.

THE UNEXPECTED MAIL ORDER BRIDE

HANNAH WINSTONE

Carolyn's feet treaded carefully as she crept from the house. She flinched with every breath, every creak of the wooden floor beneath her feet, heartbeat ringing in her ears. Once she left this place, Carolyn would be free - but first she had to actually make it out.

The front door was old and rusted, the wood warped within it's frame. Carolyn's hands were damp with sweat as she reached to turn the key within the lock. The door shuddered, lurching open with a dull creak that echoed throughout the silent house. She froze, breath caught in her throat - but nobody arrived. The occupants continued to sleep soundly, unaware of the short, dishevelled woman about to flee.

When she stepped outside, the first thing Carolyn noticed was the breeze. It whipped her hair about her face and stung her nose, but it felt so good she didn't even care. How long had it been since she had enjoyed something so simple? Weeks, at the very least. She hadn't been able to truly appreciate anything since her husband died, and then her mother-in-law had made everything worse...

No. There was no sense in self pity. Carolyn had her bag, everything important crammed inside, and she had her freedom. It was all she needed. Hefting the bag over her shoulders, she began to walk. This late at night the streets were empty, lit by flickering oil lamps that provided only a weak, sallow light. Carolyn wandered without any real idea of where to go - this late the train station would be empty, without trains to take her out of here. There were inns, but staying to morning risked being discovered.

She had planned her escape so well, focused on just getting out, that she had no idea what to do now that she had escaped.

At the very least she could get out of town. Turning a sharp left, Carolyn strode down the vacant streets, away from her home, away from the town square and everything she knew. Soon enough cramped houses turned to neat little cottages, which in turn became nothing but fields for miles. Carolyn had no idea how long she walked, not even when her feet grew tired and her joints began to ache.

Pausing for breath, Carolyn dropped her bag into the cold ground and stretched her arms. Her shoulders cracked uncomfortably, glad for a break from the weight pressing down on them. Her entire body felt bruised - her arms from carrying that heavy bag, her feet and ankles from tripping over the uneven road. How much longer until the next town over? Perhaps she could-

Her thoughts were cut off by the thud of hooves in the distance. They echoed throughout the quiet night, growing louder and louder by the second. Carolyn turned, brows raised - only to see the dim shape of an enormous caravan creeping into view. It was pulled by two dark roan horses, and the caravan itself was patterned in brilliant red and black. Carolyn darted back to let it past - but instead it rolled to a stop.

The woman riding dropped the reins and leaned across the coachman's seat. She had thick, dark hair and big brown eyes, her smile kind. "What's a young woman like you doing out here alone?"

Carolyn winced, but had no energy to be annoyed. It was expected for this woman to be curious, considering it was midnight and she was out here alone. "Just trying to get to the next town," she answered quietly.

"Why that's... well its several hours, and that's with a horse. Come inside, we can take you there?"

"We?"

"My family are inside, too. Come, please." The woman beckoned her closer, a gentle smile spread across her features.

Usually, Carolyn was smart enough not to climb into carriages with strangers. Before now, the need to do so had never come up. Yet she was exhausted, her legs ached, and she felt terrible. So against her better judgement, Carolyn took the woman's offered hand and climbed inside.

Considering the exterior, the caravan was decorated simpler than expected. It was the perfect miniature home, complete with a wide bed in the corner, concealed by curtains that were partially pulled back.

There was a sofa and an armchair, a table bolted to the floor, and even a tiny fireplace that was currently burnt to embers.

Two children sat on the bed - a slender, somewhat gangly boy and a younger girl, both with freckles splashed across their face. A man sat between them, brushing out the girl's long hair.

The woman smiled and urged Carolyn forward. "This young lady would like to travel with us until we reach the next town. How about we make some tea and make some space for her, hmm?"

The man stood - and he was so tall that his head almost bumped the ceiling. "It's nice to meet you; you can call me Enoch. As my wife forgot to tell you, her name is Oshina."

The woman - Oshina - rolled her eyes, already busying herself with adding logs to the fire. "Introductions have never been my strong suit - but anyway, what's your name?"

"Carolyn," she murmured. Still standing by the entrance - which consisted of a solid door and thick curtains - she felt so out of place. This family were clearly travellers, used to the road; Carolyn had never so much as left her hometown for a holiday. Shifting, she cast her gaze across the little caravan. It was cosy and sweet, and she had to admit she saw the appeal.

The little girl climbed from the bed, tossing hair over her shoulder. "Miss, why were you alone so early in the morning?"

"Oh," Carolyn replied. Well, there was no sense in lying. "Well, my husband died many months ago, and my mother-in-law, she... wanted me to marry her other son, instead."

The girl's nose wrinkled, "that's mean! I'm sorry your husband died."

"Now Elvira, stop pestering the poor woman. Her business is her own." Oshina hauled an enormous kettle onto the fire, turning to stare at her two children. "Now, you and Silas need to sleep, so go on. It's time for adults to talk."

The two children grumbled and moaned, but did as they were told. There was another curtained off area she hadn't noticed before, where two child-sized beds were crammed side by side. They climbed into the beds and drew the curtains. Then silence fell over the caravan.

"You're welcome to stay with us as long as you need," Oshina said kindly, "be that the next town, or the one after that."

Somehow, Carolyn managed a smile - and for the first time in a while, things felt okay.

***

Carolyn had to sleep on the sofa that night, but it was plush and warm and surprisingly comfortable. They had parked by the side of the road - not ideal, Enoch claimed, but better than some places they'd been forced to stop.

When she drifted back to consciousness, rolling onto her side and brushing thick red hair from her face, they were already on the move again. The rhythmic turning of the wheels was somewhat soothing, even as it jostled her on the narrow seat. Sitting up, she glanced around.

Suddenly a plate was shoved onto her lap, a cup placed between her palms. "Breakfast," Oshina chirped, "I hope porridge and honey is all right?"

"Perfect, thank you." Carolyn glanced down, inhaling the sweet scent of the porridge mixed with the coffee in her cup, and her stomach growled in response. Cheeks flushing, she took a hefty gulp of coffee.

"We're hoping to make it to the next town over by midday," Oshina said as he settled down in the opposite chair. "But one of our wheels has been giving us trouble, so we might stop for maintenance."

Before long, the children joined them - little Elvira watched Carolyn curiously the entire time she ate. Her big, dark eyes remained unblinking. Silas was a few years older at least, and didn't seem to care much about the curiosity of a stranger sharing their space. They both ate quickly, and then disappeared back behind the curtains to dress.

"Have you spare clothes?" Elvira asked as she finished her coffee, "I'm sure I can find you something that will fit."

Carolyn glanced at her bag, which had been left by the caravan's door overnight. "I've got some clothes," she replied quietly, "just whatever I could fit, really." It had been difficult to leave everything else behind. Carolyn had been forced to abandon her favourite books, all of the ornaments her parents had given her, even her wedding dress was still in the closet back home. Back there, because it wasn't home any more.

Oshina lay a gentle hand on her shoulder, smile gentle. "I don't know what you went through, and it's none of our business, but know that we will look out for you. In our community, we look after people."

Warmth bloomed in her chest, and Carolyn couldn't help the nervous laughter that left her lips. How was it that these strangers, people she had barely met, had offered her more than her own in-laws? They had hated her from the beginning, her mother and father in-law. When Anthony died they used it as an excuse to bully her, to make her feel useless. Then Anthony's brother had decided he wanted her for himself - and well, he always got what he wanted in the end.

Not this time.

"If you ever want to talk about it," Oshina said kindly, "I'm an excellent listener. If you don't, that's all right too," she added with a smile. She was the opposite of Carolyn's mother, all dark hair and slender build, where Mother had been bright blond and a little stocky. Oshina was younger, too. Yet there was something about her - perhaps her smile or the way she tilted her head when she spoke - that was reminiscent of her nonetheless.

Ducking her head, Carolyn set down her now empty bowl and turned her gaze to the door. With the curtains drawn back she could see through the little window - a bright blue sky rolled past, dotted with fluffy white clouds. "Thank you, but it's.. it's still to raw."

"I understand."

Although Carolyn parted her lips to say something else, she never had the chance to voice her thoughts. The caravan shuddered, the whole thing rocking perilously, and Carolyn let out a squeak as she tumbled into the sofa.

The kids laughed and jeered - but Oshina's face had gone ashy pale. "Enoch?" she called, "what's wrong?"

The caravan rolled to a complete stop, still rocking gently even as it ceased to travel. Silence filled it - thick and tense, weighing down on Carolyn like a physical force.

Enoch broke the silence first, peeking his head through the door with a sheepish sigh. "Wheel's broken," he murmured, "snapped off completely. The good news is, there's a ranch right ahead of us."

One by one they all clambered out, turning to gaze at their surroundings. Sure enough, Enoch had managed to guide the horses - and caravan - onto a dirt path. The path led to a solitary farmhouse surrounded by beautiful green fields and towering trees.

"I'll see if anyone's in," Enoch said as he dusted off his shirt, "maybe someone could help with repairs." He ambled off down the dirt path, heading straight for the house.

"Should we follow?" Carolyn suggested quietly, "what if they're rude, or don't want us here..."

Oshina was already ushering the children back inside, her face pinched in concern. Yet when she glanced at Enoch's disappearing figure, she smiled. "He'll be fine. My husband has his charm, and he's good with strangers. There's no need to worry."

Yet Carolyn did, because it was embedded in her very bones. She had always been a worrier, the type to overthink and panic - Anthony had always said it it worried him, how easily she could spiral. Shaking her head, Carolyn forced out a sigh and ran a hand through her hair. It somewhat helped, making herself breathe deeply.

Enoch was still gone long enough to make concern rise in her chest, her gaze fixed on the path ahead. Yet soon enough he returned, a second figure trotting along beside him. Said figure turned out to be a tall, well built man with bright green eyes. He looked young, perhaps only Carolyn's age, but the scowl across his face made him look much older.

"This caravan is in bad state," he murmured, apparently more to himself than anybody else. "how did the wheel come off?"

"It's an old thing," Enoch replied defensively, "it's lasted us many decades."

The man's nose wrinkled, but his eyes lost some of their harshness. "It will take work - why don't you come inside and get warm first?"

Oshina was all too eager to comply, fetching the children and sending them running off ahead. "Only to the porch!" she called after them, then turned to the man with an apologetic smile, "They're at that age where they're nothing but energy. Apologies, Mr...?"

"Just David is fine," he answered with a shrug.

The four of them traipsed back to the house, where the children waited by the front door. The house itself was modest, clean yet scarcely furnished. There were no photographs or paintings on the wall, no ornaments or clutter taking up shelves. Even the kitchen, as David took them in, was basic. There wasn't so much as a newspaper lying on the table.

"I'll make tea," David offered, "have you eaten yet?"

"We had breakfast not long ago," Enoch answered, "but it wasn't much as we haven't restocked."

"Then I'll make eggs and bacon."

"And I'll go back to have a look at the caravan," Enoch replied with a frown. Climbing to his feet, he disappeared into the hall.

With David focused on the meal and Oshina entirely occupied with the children, Carolyn was at a loss of what to do. She perched awkwardly on the nearest chair, twirling a loose strand of hair around her finger. She found herself watching David as he cooked, admiring how delicately he cracked the eggs into the bowl. Eventually she stood, coming to his side. "Do you need help with that?"

He watched her from the corner of his eyes, but didn't turn his head to face her. "You could fill the kettle and fetch the teapot, please. Cupboard to your left."

Eager to be helpful, Carolyn darted to fetch the kettle. It was a huge metal thing that made her arms ache to lift up, but she managed to drop it not too inelegantly onto the hearth. Then she hefted the teapot from the cupboard above the sink, setting it on the table for later. It was almost entirely white, the teapot, save for a delicate silver pattern that wound around the base. It was far more ornate than she would have expected, given the simplicity of the rest of the house - and it looked brand new. As if it had been a gift for someone, but David had decided to use it himself.

Wandering back over to the kitchen counter, something flashed in her vision. A letter, tucked beneath the bread bin. She only caught a glimpse of the name Mary-Anne before David leaned across to get the bread, blocking her view.

"Do you live here alone?" Carolyn questioned.

His eyes narrowed curiously. "I do. Why?"

"That letter, from Mary-Anne-"

"Mary-Anne isn't any of your business," he snapped, "so I suggest you leave it alone."

Carolyn pursed her lips, eyes going wide. Even the children had stopped bickering, turning their wide gaze to stare openly at David. Silence filled the room, nobody daring to speak first. Not even Carolyn, despite how guilt swelled in her chest.

Moments passed, and eventually David huffed out a sigh. "If you must know, Mary-Anne was to be my wife. She was from California, but never made it here. Now, you don't need to know any more - you are guests, and this is my home." Without another word, he turned his back on Carolyn to place a heavy pan over the flames, where the bacon began to sizzle.

Carolyn and Oshina shared a wide-eyed look, but said nothing. Frankly, Carolyn had no idea what to make of David. He had invited them into his home, offered them help, and then treated them like a burden. His motivations were a mystery, if he had any at all.

The meal passed in awkward silence, with even little Elvira unwilling to speak. Enoch arrived back inside to join them, and by his uncomfortable fidgeting he noticed the atmosphere, too. By the time everyone had finished eating, the silence had stretched on for so long that nobody was willing to break it.

It wasn't until later that Carolyn caught David outside, looking over the caravan with a scowl. She came to a stop beside him, staring down at the broken wheel. Broken didn't describe it properly - smashed was more like it. It had broken into half a dozen pieces, and the underneath of the caravan had suffered damage because of it.

"It's going to take days to fix," David huffed, "this caravan should have been retired years ago."

Biting down on her lip, Carolyn only shrugged. "They obviously love it," she replied quietly, "but I didn't come here to talk about the caravan."

"Then what?"

Why was he so difficult to talk to? Yes, he was a stranger - but Oshina was a stranger too, and she had been nothing but lovely. Was David naturally this rude, or was it on purpose? Frowning, she said, "I'm sorry, for earlier. I had no right to bring up something personal."

"No, you didn't," David replied - yet he paused in his observations to turn to Carolyn, his features relaxing, "but it's my fault, too. I don't... get visitors. Ever. I suppose I've forgotten how to talk to people."

Sympathy twinged deep in her chest, made her heart skitter anxiously. "I'm sorry," she repeated kindly, "how about we start again? Hello, I'm Carolyn."

"David," he replied, amusement sparkling in his dark eyes.

When Carolyn saw the smile spread across his angular features, she decided perhaps he wasn't so bad after all.

***

They fell into routine, after that. Oshina cared for the children while David and Enoch worked on the caravan. Carolyn mostly tended to the horses, who had been put in the stables with David's own animals. A few days passed like this, with everyone kept too busy to talk much, until they unanimously decided to take a break.

Somehow, Carolyn found herself hovering by David as he chopped wood. "You should really take a break too," she offered, watching they way his muscles stretched beneath his shirt. He wasn't overly muscular, but David had a broad build and wide shoulders that strained the confines of his clothing.

He only huffed, bringing up a new log to chop. "I still have to take care of the ranch. Just because you need help doesn't mean I can let my normal duties go."

"Then I could help?"

He turned his gaze to Carolyn, biting down on his lip. He seemed to truly consider it for a moment, humming low in his throat - but eventually shook his head. "It's a kind offer, really, but I've been doing this for years."

"You wouldn't want a townie ruining your schedule?" Carolyn offered with a smile. She was more useful than he gave her credit for, but he was right in one respect - Carolyn would only have slowed him down. Sighing, she turned to cast her gaze across the ranch. In the mid-afternoon sun everything was a shade of soft yellow-gold, giving the fields an ethereal look. Dreamlike. Despite the hard work it took to keep a ranch going, she understood the charm.

She turned back to David, feeling more relaxed than she had in weeks - only to see him doubled over in pain. With a hand pressed to his chest he let out a rumbling cough, one that came from deep inside his lungs. In the time it took Carolyn to dart forward, that cough turned to heavy, gasping hacks as David struggled to stay upright.

Without thinking, Carolyn scooped an arm around his waist and eased him to the ground. He didn't even try to fight her, whole body shaking as they sank into the grass together. Heart pounding, Carolyn could only watch in muted horror, her own breathing coming in fast, sharp gasps. "What do you need?" she demanded, but he only waved her off. "David, look at me. What do you need?"

He waved her off again, eyes narrowed as he glared at Carolyn. The coughing died down soon enough, however, leaving him red-faced and breathless, but apparently unharmed. Taking in slow, deep breaths, David still didn't sound like he was breathing right.

"What happened?" Carolyn demanded. Her heart was still thundering against her ribcage, pulse painfully hot. She reached out for him, anxiety turning in her gut, only to be shaken off. "Do you need a doctor?"

"Doctor's won't help," David snapped - but as breathless as he was, there was no venom to his voice. Taking in another struggling breath, he added, "I've been ill my whole life, no point in trying to fix it now."

Ill? An illness was the flu or a stomach bug, but this was worse. She had seen him there, unable to breath as he coughed up his lungs. Yet he made it sound so normal, as if it was just a part of every day life.

She must have been staring, because David turned to shoot her a narrow-eyed glare. He was handsome even then, although the intensity of it worried her. "You want to know what's wrong with me, don't you?"

Well, yes. Could she be blamed for that? Cheeks flushed, Carolyn simply nodded.

"I was born with weak lungs," he answered coolly, "so if I get too cold or too hot, or overwork myself... well, breathing can get difficult. It isn't usually this bad, but with the summer coming in and the extra work I've taken on..." he trailed off with a shrug. "It always passes, but it gets more difficult each time."

Oh. Guilt rose in Carolyn's chest, pain making her heart lurch. He was worse because of them. because of the strain fixing the caravan had caused. "Will you..?" she couldn't even finish the sentence.

"Die?" He laughed, but the sound was humourless. Rolling his eyes, David shifted so he was sitting straighter, his back cracking with each movement. "Not today, and probably not soon - but eventually? Yes. It will kill me."

Carolyn winced, those words hitting her deeply. What must it have been like, knowing every day that the end was coming? Few people knew when they were going to die, but to know it was closer for you than it was for others... it must have been painful in a different way. Blinking back tears, Carolyn wiped a hand across her face.

"Now don't go crying," David huffed - although there was a smile in his voice, "I've done better than expected - the first doctor said I wouldn't live past twelve."

"And how old are you now?" she asked without thinking.

"Twenty-two."

That put him at a year older than Carolyn herself, who had only just turned twenty-one. Why did that thought bring a smile to her face? It didn't matter how old David was, it wasn't even her business. Yet a smile did curl a the edge of her lips, and she let out a sigh. "Are you sure you'll be all right?" she asked again, "maybe you should rest."

David simply rolled his eyes, climbing to his feet. His breath was still uneven, but for the most part he sounded recovered. "Would you like the caravan fixed, or not?"

"Well, yes."

"Then I'll continue."

Unwilling to argue, Carolyn simply sat back and watched him work.

***

The porch was too small, really, for everyone to crowd onto at once. Yet the sun was beautiful this evening, already beginning to set as it cast pink rays across the fields, and it had been too lovely to stay shut indoors. So here they sat, all six of them, enjoying supper under the waning sun.

Carolyn held her bowl loosely in one hand, perched on the steps leading to the little dirt path. Little Elvira sat at her feed, eagerly mopping up soup with a chunk of fresh bread. She had taken a liking to the young girl, and Elvira to her, over the week they'd been together.

More than that, though, was how she had taken to David. Oshina mentioned it now, her lips parted into a smile. "You like him, don't you?"

Carolyn almost choked on her soup, turning to glare at Oshina with narrowed blue eyes. "He's right there," she hissed, nodding toward where the two men sat. They remained oblivious, talking silently amongst each other. It brought her a little relief, to know nobody was eavesdropping.

Oshina's expression turned sympathetic, a smile gracing her pretty features. Her voice was motherly as she said, "he's a good man. Strange, and a little detached, but good at heart. You could certainly do worse."

She made it sound like... like they were courting. Carolyn didn't want to think about why that made her chest stutter, or why she suddenly wanted to smile. Sinking deeper into her cardigan, she simply sighed. "All right. Yes, I do like David - he's been kind to us, even if he is difficult. He's charming, too, when he wants to be."

"But?" Oshina prompted with a smile. Her own unfinished meal sat beside her, no longer relevant now that there was a story to hear. Apparently, Carolyn was more interesting than food.

Cringing, Carolyn forced herself to take a bite. Her own appetite was minimal at the best of times, never mind when she was being interrogated about her feelings. "I've been widowed before, Oshina.

My husband died and it left me with nothing. I won't go through that again."

"Everyone dies eventually," Oshina replied quietly. She cast a nervous glance toward the two men, where Silas played beside them, but nobody was listening. "You can't deny yourself what you want just in case something bad happens. Then you'll never do anything."

Well, when she put it like that, perhaps she had a point. Even so, Carolyn knew she couldn't go through that again. Anthony's death had ruined her, left her alone and desolate. Her parents died when she was young, caught the flu and let it go untreated. Then Anthony had died a year later, only six months after their wedding day. Carolyn had seen too much death, lost too many already.

Oshina placed a hand on her shoulder, giving it a reassuring squeeze. "I had a husband too, before Enoch. We were going to settle down, abandon the traveller life - but he died in an accident when I was only nineteen. It was awful and heart breaking, but it didn't stop me from finding love again."

At that at least, Carolyn managed a smile. "You're a braver woman than I am, then."

"I don't think so at all. We all deal with grief differently."

Movement from behind had Carolyn turning to look - and when she did, her eyes caught David's gaze. For a moment she thought he had overheard their conversation, but then he simply smiled and disappeared inside. Was it her imagination, or had his breathing sounded strained?

You're paranoid, the sensible part of her brain snapped. Yet she stood anyway, slipping inside the hall to check. Oshina watched her go, expression fond.

"David?" Carolyn called into the dark hallway. "Are you all right?"

She found him in the kitchen, a cold glass of water pressed to the side of his neck. His brows rose when he spotted her, but his smile was genuine. "Just too warm," he replied raspily, "when it gets humid like this, it's difficult."

Carolyn crossed the small space between them, dampening a kitchen rag to press it against his collarbone. "It won't help your breathing," she said, "but at least you won't melt."

"Thank you."

The sincerity in his voice surprised her, left her staring up at him with wide, unsure eyes. In the short time she had stayed with David, Carolyn had quickly learned that being nice, usually ended in sarcastic comments or offhand remarks. It very rarely ended in a genuine expression of thanks. Blinking slowly, she turned to look at him. "You're welcome."

They stood there for a long moment, eyes locked. David's were a bright, rich green like the fields he lived near. How had she never noticed the little flecks of brown before? They were beautiful, and-

Her thoughts were cut off as lips met hers. They were rough and chapped but somehow still so soft, perhaps because of how gentle they were. David smelled of warm hay and fresh bread, his lips were pliable as he leaned into the kiss. Carolyn was lost in him, her vision tunnelling until all that mattered was them.

She broke from him with a gasp that caught in her throat - and then she shoved him away, darting backwards until her back pressed against the wall.

"I'm sorry," David replied, "I should have asked-"

"I can't do this," Carolyn cut in with a stuttering gasp. She sounded worse than David himself, her breath catching in her throat, "I've lost enough loved ones in my life."

Before David could answer she spun on here heel, vision wavering, and darted off into the hall. Everyone else was still outside and so she took the back door, flying into the darkness without looking back. It wasn't until David's voice faded into the background that she stopped to suck in great breaths, hands on her knees.

It didn't matter what Oshina had said - Carolyn refused to lose someone else. If that meant never having them in the first place, then so be it.

***

The caravan was finally fixed, and the family were eager to be on their way. Already Enoch was readying the horses, Oshina gathering up the children to send them inside. They looked so delighted to have their caravan back, and it warmed Carolyn's heart.

"Carolyn," Oshina called from inside the caravan, "do you have all of your things ready?"

Glancing down at her bag, the last of the items she owned, Carolyn sighed. She had expected to be excited now, to be glad to be on the road again - but all she felt was dull disappointment at the thought of leaving. She had nowhere to go, no plans for her new life, and hardly anything to her name. Wherever she went, it would be the same problem.

"Carolyn?" Oshina popped her head through the caravan's door - and upon seeing Carolyn, her expression softened. Climbing down, she approached her. "You don't want to come with us, do you?"

"It isn't that," she answered honestly - because Oshina was wonderful, and she had such an amazing family, how could Carolyn not want to be with them? "It's just... I can't bear to leave on such bad terms with David."

Pursing her lips, Oshina cast a long look across the ranch. The man in question stood by the porch, watching them prepare to leave, and her gaze hovered just a moment too long. Carolyn herself couldn't even look at him. "He'll understand, dear. But I know that you'll never forgive yourself if you don't make things right - so what are you waiting for?"

"He doesn't want to talk to me. After the way I rejected him, he must want me gone." Cheeks flared, Carolyn ducked her head. Her chest ached to speak with him, and a part of her longed to hold him, but she couldn't. Carolyn had lost any right to want those things, after the way she had treated him.

Oshina's eyes flickered between Carolyn and the distant figure of David. "You won't know until you try. Take a risk?"

Nose crinkling, Carolyn let out a soft sigh. Once, Carolyn wouldn't have hesitated to do such a thing - now, she couldn't bring herself to do so. It didn't matter how much she loved David, because-

Wait. Loved? The thought had popped into her head unbidden. Unprompted. Yet as the thought circled through her mind, she knew there was truth to it. They had known each other hardly any time at all, and yet... yes, she loved him.

"Go. Talk to him."

Carolyn turned, watched him as he sat on the porch steps, and she knew she couldn't leave now. "All right," she murmured, "I will."

"Good girl."

The dirt path crunched underneath her feet, the breeze carrying her forward. David glanced up as she approached, his brow knitted into a deep scowl - but Carolyn didn't let it deter her. Perhaps she had ruined things between them, by doing what she did - but she simply couldn't leave without knowing.

"Carolyn," David spoke as she neared, "I thought you would be leaving with everybody else-"

"What I did the other day was wrong. I shouldn't have reacted the way I did, and I should never have ran away from you." The words left her in a flurry, her breath catching, and once she started speaking, Carolyn couldn't stop. "David, I can't even begin to express how I feel for you, and I'm so sorry that I let my past get in the way of is. Of us."

He simply blinked, apparently unable to form a coherent thought. Or perhaps he simply thought she was being ridiculous; a thought that made her stomach drop.

"Maybe I shouldn't have said anything," Carolyn spluttered, a brilliant flush spreading across her slender cheeks, "please, forget I said anything and I can-"

Carolyn was cut off by a pair of warm, thick arms enveloping her. David pulled her close, buried his face in the crook of her neck, and inhaled like she was the best thing he had ever held. "There's no need to explain, Carolyn," he murmured against her ear, "because I understand how you feel. When I heard Mary-Anne had passed, I didn't want to get close to anyone, either. Not until you."

Warmth bloomed in her chest, a brilliant smile gracing her features. She clung to him, fingers digging into the fabric of his shirt, and let out a relieved sigh. "You mean it?"

"Of course I do. We've hardly known each other long at all, but I already know I love you."

The words struck her like a physical thing, sucking the breath from her lungs and leaving her frozen. Even Anthony, her late husband, had never expressed his love so freely. "I love you too," she murmured - and then kissed him.

Their kiss was chaste yet sweet, barely a brush of their lips, but it left her breathless, her mind fuzzy with happiness. She could have held him forever and never let go, simply enjoying the feel of his skin against hers.

A cough from behind had them jumping apart, David's cheeks blooming a beautiful rosy pink. Carolyn righted herself, glancing down at the two standing by the porch.

Oshina's eyes sparkled in amusement, as if to say I told you so. Young Elivra, on the other hand, turned away in disgust.

"Sorry," Carolyn murmured, "did you need something?"

"We're ready to leave," Oshina replied with a bright smile, "unless you plan on staying..?"

Carolyn turned to David, lips parted in a silent question. She couldn't expect to stay, couldn't expect David to want her permanently-

"Of course you can stay," David answered her unasked question, his smile a brilliant white, "you belong here as much as I do."

Grinning so widely her mouth ached, Carolyn kissed him once again.

An Amish Widow's Window

21

Amanda Roxley

Chapter 1: Flashbacks

Falling in love can happen all at once and also over a long period of time. Some people say that there is only one moment, and in that moment, you know that you've fallen in love. Falling in love, for Elizabeth, happened more or less, by accident. Elizabeth Brenneman fell in love suddenly yet slowly at the same time. His name was James Harper. She was sitting inside the Neptune Diner on the corner of Pine and Orange Streets with some of her new English girlfriends when James Harper arrived on the scene. James was the boyfriend of Megan Sanchez, a short plumpy Latino girl, with thick dark brown girls. She was also endowed with a generous chest, an amazing smile, and a silly laugh. When James came to the diner at 1 am in the morning and sat down by Megan, Elizabeth liked him immediately, but never thought she would fall in love with James. Why?

·James was Megan's boyfriend,

·James was an Englishman.

·She was/is(?) Amish.

·Elizabeth was an honest girl.

·James was wrong for Elizabeth in every way.

·James had a huge tattoo on his left shoulder (and Elizabeth didn't care for the Englishmen's tattoos.)

Elizabeth loved the Lord, and she never wanted to fall into a path that led to dishonesty, cheating, or leaving her family. She didn't cheat, actually, but it felt like it. While Elizabeth was experiencing Rumspringa, a time when Amish youth are allowed to enter the "modern world" and decide if they want to remain Amish, she found herself taking a liking to the English dance styles. Every Friday night

Elizabeth and her new English friends would go to a local Christian church hall and take part in something called contra dancing. Contra dancing occurred in a square formation, but you also danced with your partner and up and down the hall in lines with another set of partners simultaneously. In fact, it was quite difficult to explain what contra was or why she loved it, but she did, nonetheless. Elizabeth wasn't quite used to dancing with so many people, but it was fun, and she loved the music. There was an array of sounds that filled the air; delicate, yet elaborate wooden instruments with strings produced a sound that she had never heard before. The people dressed in long, flowy skirts, in bright oranges, blues, pinks, and even reds, as they danced across the hall with a grace that she longed to achieve.

Although Elizabeth usually arrived without a date to the local Friday night contra dancing, one night Megan said she could not go dancing and it wasn't a problem if she went with James. Elizabeth considered what a quandary that put her in...if she was in her Amish community this would never happen. Of course, a lot of things would never happen, such as dancing, going out on a Friday night, or drinking a milkshake at 1 am at the local diner. She loved all of it and hated all of it at the same time because Rumspringa showed her a whole new world, but that world did not include her family, and it did include James and Meg.

From the night that Elizabeth and James danced together, Elizabeth felt a spark in her heart that no Amish man had ever given her. She felt the feeling of being light on her feet, a feeling that could hardly be described with words. When he smiled at her nothing could keep a smile off her face. Since the evening that Elizabeth and James danced together, the two kept their feelings under lock and key regarding their unspoken attraction. Megan, however, saw that James was into Elizabeth and perhaps Elizabeth was interested in James too, so she broke-up with James even though she liked him. In some strange way, Megan gave them her blessing and saw their relationship all the way to the altar.

Even as Elizabeth uttered the words, "I do, she felt her heart break in two. Her life forever was divided. Her heart, well, was even more so divided. Her decision to wed James came with the decision to leave her family. Now, she found herself even more torn and heartbroken, because she was without James. She received the phone call when she was sitting at home sewing little booties for their baby on the way. James' boss, Marshall Hoover, called from the bar, where James worked as a bartender. Marshall started speaking slowly in a hushed tone. That was when Elizabeth knew that something was wrong. Elizabeth always knew Marshall, in the short time she had known him, to be a man who spoke his mind, and didn't hold back.

The conversation came back to Elizabeth in pieces. She still couldn't remember all of it. There had been an accident... James wasn't feeling very well when he came into work.... James looked pale... he was pouring drinks... and then he collapsed on the floor. A bar patron called 911, but by the time the ambulance arrived he was already gone. Elizabeth kept running the phone call through her head as if somehow it would change things or bring James back. James had suffered a fatal heart attack. They didn't know that James had a heart condition, but apparently, he did. He was too young to die. She was too young to be a widow. But she was. Elizabeth Brenneman was a widow.

Chapter 2: Not the Only Broken Heart

Elizabeth Brenneman was not the only one with a broken heart. More than one fellow yearned to marry Elizabeth Brenneman and was devastated when Elizabeth unexpectedly fell in love on Rumspringa. Elizabeth was the kind of girl you knew would be a loving, caring wife, and a sweet and tender mother. Any young Amish boy would dream of being Elizabeth's husband up until the point when Elizabeth left the community for James. Although the Amish community agreed that it was too bad that Elizabeth's husband had died so suddenly and at such a young age, there were not so many suitors that were still in interested in Elizabeth. Who would want to marry a young pregnant widow with a baby on the way?

Elizabeth did not feel the need to marry again, but she did feel the fear of raising her baby boy alone. Three weeks after James died, she found herself at Lancaster Women and Babies' Hospital. She was pushing, pushing, with only Megan by her side. Megan remained dedicated to Elizabeth, out of love and also of a sense of duty, because she allowed and even encouraged Elizabeth to date James. Little did she know she would be next to Elizabeth's side without James, as she birthed her child. After James Brenneman was born, Elizabeth found herself unable to care for her own child. She felt that giving her boy, his father's name would give him a sense of pride one day, but she also wanted to honor her Amish heritage and gave her boy her own last name.

The problem with giving birth and grieving a dead husband at the same time was that it was simply impossible. James looked like his father which made it harder and easier at the same time. James Junior had a round face, with olive skin and a small tuft of dark brown hair on the top of his head. He made everyone smile and laugh, and even though Elizabeth was eligible to receive financial support from the government she did not want to raise her boy in the English word without his father. She chose to leave her home for her husband, but without her husband, Elizabeth suffered. Whatever glow James put in her step was taken away by his death. There was only one true option, returning home, destined to remain a widow for the rest of her life.

She feared the reaction of her parents who were naturally crushed when she told them she fell in love and wanted to marry an Englishmen. When her husband died that night in the bar serving drinks she couldn't even think to tell her parents. Her father rejected her when she left and couldn't handle the thought of Elizabeth leaving the family, her home, their home, the community. It took Elizabeth over a month after his death to send a message to her parents through a friend that he passed away. She never heard a response from her parents and assumed that they did not want anything to do with her again. That was certainly more than fair considering what she had done. Sometimes she wondered if God was punishing her for marrying James? Wasn't God a good God? A fair God? A just God? A loving God? Surely the God that she learned about from her family and her community would not want her to be like this. To be broken hearted and alone. She would return. She would go back and then what? Only God knew.

Chapter 3: Strange English Ways

There was a community meeting to decide the fate of the young and no longer naïve Elizabeth and her newborn son, James. Her parents seemed to be unable to face her return as it would bring shame to their family, and her former friends and neighbors did not want to say anything against the Brenneman family for fear that they would lose even their respect. In a strange way, even though the Brennnemans did not want to respect the request of their daughter to return with her son, nobody wanted to speak in favor of Elizabeth, except one, Wayne Bender.

Wayne Bender was not an important man in the community, but he was a male voice, and in the Amish community, elders and men received the most respect. Wayne had a strong, solid, sounding voice that echoed through the hall. "Do we not preach forgiveness? Do we not believe in giving the homeless a home? Do we not believe in clothing the naked? Do we not believe in caring for the sick?" asked Wayne. The Beatitudes were what Wayne preached. "How could we call ourselves the children of God if we turn against one of our own in her time of need? Can we deny the needs of her newborn son?" roared Wayne through the town hall.

There were murmurs among the people until one by one the townspeople agreed with Wayne. How could they forsake Elizabeth?

Even though her own parents were not quick to forgive, for certain, she was in her hour of need, as was her son. With Wayne's words, the community softened and agreed that something could be done. Finally, one of the elderly women in the community, Mary, stood up and spoke on her behalf. "Elizabeth and her boy can live in my spare shed that I'm not using anymore. It's not really a fit living space, but I hate to see a girl on the street with a little one. I would need some help to make it a livable area, a bed for the girl, a crib for the little boy, and a proper toilet and sink. I suppose it could really use a new coat of paint and the windows are a little loose too. They make an awful rattling sound in the wind," she stated.

Slowly others chimed in. "Mary, if you have the space, I can help you with the labor," said Mary's son, Solomon. Wayne immediately agreed that he could help with renovations too. Slowly, but surely, the voices of those wanting to help Elizabeth were much greater than those who remained silent or in objection. "Actually, my husband knows plumbing, I bet he can connect a toilet outdoors," said another neighbor. So, it was decided that they would accept the return of Elizabeth and her son, despite the situation being extremely unusual, and the fact that typically those who chose to leave the Amish community were never permitted to return.

Meanwhile, Elizabeth sat with her son James in her and her former husband's apartment in shock. As tears rolled down her cheek she caressed her sweet son's face. Everything about James reminded her of her husband. How could it be possible that God allowed her to be in this position? If God was so loving then why did bad things happen to good people? She saw so much of her husband was in her young son including his pleasant demeanor. The one thing that Elizabeth had to be thankful for was her son's never-ending smiles and his ability to sleep through the night. She started attending a widow's support group in the city, but went only twice, after she realized that all the attendees were at least over the age of 60, and Elizabeth was barely

22. The moderator of the support group, a soft-spoken elderly woman, Josefine Reagan, caught Elizabeth on the way out the door the second and last time she attended the group.

"My dear, I know you are hurting, I wish there was something I could do for you, and I see that you are struggling. I know this group, well... we just aren't quite your age group, but you're welcome to go to Water Street Rescue Mission. There they help a lot of people in need. They have even depression support groups and single mother's groups. I hope I'm not offending you my dear, and of course you're still more than welcome to come here, but I think there you might find what you are looking for," said Josefine, as she handed Elizabeth a pamphlet with the address and phone number of the Water Street Rescue Mission on it.

"Thanks, I appreciate it really, said Elizabeth as tears rolled down her face. Despite trying to control her emotions she couldn't help but feel everything. Why did she have to feel everything? Everything. Everything was okay before Rumspringa. She began to feel an anger building up inside her, a feeling that she was not used to experiencing. Anger. It's just a stage of grief. That's what the therapist at the hospital had told her after James had passed away. The therapist, much like everyone else, handed her a card with her phone number on it and offered support, but whatever support the modern English word could offer could not compare with what support her home community would offer her if they accepted her back.

Elizabeth almost forgot that she was still standing in front of Josefine due to her scattered thoughts. She bid her goodbye and gave her an awkward half-hug before walking away. She did not turn around or even look at the woman's eyes. Josefine was doing the best she could, but Elizabeth knew already the support group was not going to be able to help her in any way. These women wanted to sit and sew and spew out good memories of all the years they spent with their husbands, of what their grown adult-age children were doing now, and how they enjoyed still being a part of the church, singing in the choir, cleaning the pews and dusting the statues.

While listening to the English widows speak, she longed for her own church community and a proper upbringing for her son. As she reached her apartment door she knew she was already resolved to return if they would have her back. She crumpled up the Water Street Rescue Mission pamphlet with her right hand and threw it on the ground as she turned the key to her apartment with her left hand. She wondered if her little boy would be left-handed like herself or right-handed like her father. Amidst her thoughts, she decided that even though her parents never returned her message but she would go, nonetheless.

Chapter 4: Healing Takes a Lifetime

Megan and Elizabeth sat together in the same diner where Elizabeth first met James, each drinking a coffee. Megan wanted Elizabeth to remember something special and at least their friendship. As a gesture of their friendship and where they came from, Megan asked Elizabeth to come out of her apartment and meet her one last time at the diner for "old time's sake." Elizabeth brought little James Junior in tow on her back. Elizabeth ordered her favorite breakfast for dinner, something that would typically never be allowed in her community. This was, after all, supposed to be a celebration of friendship. Not everything could be gray skies and tears forever.

Crispy hash browns, a Belgian waffle smothered a butter and sugary syrup, four slices of beef bacon, and a glass of apple juice. For certain this meal was a sin, but they were all of Elizabeth's favorite English breakfast foods. She had never seen so many carbohydrates that tasted so good yet so different from the flavors of home. She could not imagine her mother connecting electricity to the house, let alone using a waffle iron like the ones they used in the diner. For a few moments, Elizabeth found her laughing and smiling with Meg and baby James.

Meg asked Elizabeth, "Do you remember when I brought James to the diner, and you met him for the first time?" "How could I forget?" asked Elizabeth, somewhat happy and somewhat sad to be reminded of her dead husband. "You know girl, if you were anybody else, I would have called you a boyfriend stealer!" shouted Meg, a little louder than necessary. The waitress glared at Meg a little but none of the customers raised their heads even a little or dared to look at the two girls and the baby at the table by the window, creating more noise than usual. Their usual waitress was absent and she would never have said a thing, as she knew everything, well... almost everything about their lives. Regardless, Elizabeth attempted to shush Meg, which made the two only laugh louder. Not to mention that milk squirted through Meg's noise and went all over the table.

After an hour or so Elizabeth found herself reminded of her new responsibilities and her new life. "Meg, really, thank you so much, for everything, I mean it, but you know I have to go back," said Elizabeth. "I know," said Meg. "I love you, really, but James and I... we need a family. We are a family, but we have to go back. It's time for this little kiddo to meet his grandparents. I hope they want to meet us," stated Elizabeth. "You know girl, you got some courage!" said Meg. "Let's hit the road, shall we?" asked Elizabeth. "Damn, girl, you are practically an 'English lady' already. You and your non-Amish phrases like, 'let's hit the road.' I'm gonna miss you toots!" pronounced Meg.

As the two left the room, Elizabeth glanced around the diner, took mental snapshots in her mind of the room, her friendship with Meg, and even the food. She looked down at baby James, cooed him to sleep, and the two took off in the car for one last ride in the country together. Although they hoped it wouldn't be the last, they had to be a bit realistic. The wind wiped in circles around their bodies. Meg felt the time slipping away as the sun dipped below the horizon. Reds mixed with oranges colored the sky. Tall corn stalks dotted the countryside and the radio played Sia's "*No Cheap Thrills*," as they curved around Lancaster County's corners. For a moment, just a moment, Elizabeth laughed a true laugh.

Chapter 5: Whatever Shall Come, Will Come

Wayne stood in front of Mary's shed and considered all the work that would need to be done in order to make it livable for a young mother like Elizabeth. It certainly wasn't a palace, but it could be home with the help of the community. In the end, about 60% of the community had agreed to pitch in materials and labor to make the shed a home for Elizabeth and James Junior. Elizabeth's parents, however, remained silent on the matter, as they suffered from their own struggle of having felt rejected from their daughter when she chose to marry an Englishman. After all, who could blame them for having more than mixed feelings about their daughter's expected return? Although Elizabeth had not explicitly stated that she would return it was understood by her message to her parents that this was the best possible outcome for her and her newborn.

While Elizabeth struggled with the thought of raising James alone and the possible innumerable number of reactions her parents could have to her request to returning to the community, Wayne assembled a building crew. Wayne gathered some of the community's best painters, plumbers, wood workers, and gardeners. Fortunately for Elizabeth, it was the growing season and if seeds were planted now Elizabeth would at least have a wide array of fruits and vegetables ready for her to eat in the summer, and she could freeze anything she could not eat.

One of the best things about the Amish community was how they stood together in solidarity. As Elizabeth was packing her bags and negotiating the remaining payment on the lease with her landlord, Wayne and his assembled team added an extra small room to the shed. They knocked out a wall and created a bedroom for Elizabeth and her son. In the main "room" someone had donated a wood-burning stove and another community member donated an armchair. Quickly the additional room was added to the shed, which was to be Elizabeth's new home. Behind the shed, a few of the woman worked the land, turned the soil, and planted seeds so that Elizabeth could have an abundance of food in a few months. A plumber installed an outdoor toilet in an adjacent building, and within the day the space looked like someone could actually like there. It was no longer just a place for sheep, ox, and or even a working man's tools. It was a home.

Wayne, however, had another interest in helping Elizabeth, besides his altruistic reason. Since he was no more than 15 he had his eyes on Elizabeth. Never, never, in a thousand years could he have imagined that Elizabeth would fall in love with an Englishman while on Rumspringa, nor, could he believe that perhaps he was getting his second chance to be with Elizabeth. He desired so much to be with her and also to be a father. Someone needed to be a father to the little boy, and even if she would not have her, James needed a man in his life to teach him about life and to show him the ways of the world, not just the Amish world, but also even the English world. He should be able to make his own decision one day about whether or not he wanted to return to the English world of his father or stay Amish. Undoubtedly, Elizabeth would want her son to be baptized in the church when she returned.

Wayne was counting on her returning. How would he explain to the community that they had prepared a place for her and her newborn to live if she never came back? Wayne resolved that, as per Amish custom, all things had to be determined with a calm mind and a steady fist. Since he had neither of those at the moment, he made his way to his father's house to see if he was okay. Ever since his mother died, his father struggled to feel himself. Even though he always appeared to be himself to the public, he knew that on the inside he struggled.

The night air was thin, the stars shined more brightly than the previous nights as there was not a cloud in sight. He remembered a multitude of nights from when he was a boy that he longed to view the stars, but the sky remained covered in clouds and blocked his beautiful view. The city of Lancaster, albeit, not a very large one, compared to other English cities, still also created light pollution that sometimes also affected his ability to see the stars. Tonight, however, was simply perfect. The stars were aligned in the sky and brightly lit as if the stars knew his deepest desires.

Chapter 6: The Birth of a New Day

Aside from a few sentimental items and several English gadgets that Elizabeth decided to keep, she more or less abandoned her English life. Her husband's watch and wedding ring, several English novels, fine china that was a wedding gift from Meg, wedding photos, English drink mix called Kool-Aid, and a roll of duct tape all made her suitcases but what Elizabeth could not carry in her suitcase she left to Meg. A return to her roots, to simplicity, was what she and James needed now if they were going to be okay.

As Elizabeth approached the home of her Aunt Abigail with baby James and her few belongings she felt herself shake inside with fear. She knocked lightly on the door and was relieved when her Aunt Abigail was overjoyed to see her return. "Oh, my dear, Elizabeth. I'm so sorry, I could not believe when I heard the news. This must be James Junior. What a sweet little boy you have, Liz," pronounced Elizabeth's aunt. "Oh well, I guess I can't just leave you standing on the doorstep like this, do come in," said Aunt Abigail.

"Um, Aunt Abigail, have you heard from my parents? Will they accept my return?" asked Elizabeth as she crossed the threshold of her Aunt's home. "Oh, don't worry about them, they'll come around. We're happy to have you home again. Don't listen to everything everyone says around here, you know how they are. Not everyone here agrees about anything, ever. You're not exactly new to these parts," said Aunt Abigail.

"Sorry to ask, but do you think there is a room I can nurse James?" asked Elizabeth. "It is his feeding time, and I don't want to make him wait too much longer." Elizabeth's Auntie led her down the hallway to her own bedroom, paused, opened the door just a crack, and said to her, "You know, I'm sorry we don't have enough space for you here but the community did do something for you that I think you'll like. You know who started the whole thing? That Wayne boy...he's a good boy, Elizabeth. You ought to thank him when you see him." "Oh, really," stated Elizabeth in a surprised manner. "I can't return to my parents' house?

she inquired. Not right now, Darlin', but don't you worry, everything will be okay."

After Elizabeth nursed James, Aunt Abigail recommended that they go and speak with Wayne and the owner of the small home where Elizabeth could stay. Her Aunt Abigail explained in a long-winded fashion the entire story about how nobody wanted to step up and help except Wayne, but one by one he had gained support from the majority of the community. When they arrived at the former shed which was now transformed into a miniature home, Elizabeth sighed relief and met the owner of the home. Thanking her profusely, she started to cry, thinking about where she came from and the road she had yet to cross. With tears of gratitude, she placed her bags down inside the home and gently placed James in a new crib which someone had built for her. Her tears were mixed with joy and sadness, but at least, she was home again.

The next day, Wayne came by the house to see if Elizabeth was settling into her home with James. "Good afternoon Miss Elizabeth, I see that you've made yourself at home. I just wanted to make sure you were alright since you're here alone with this cute little guy," said Wayne as he smiled at both Elizabeth and baby James. "Yes, thank you so much for everything you've done. Really, I could never have imagined that someone could do all of this for me, well, for us," replied Elizabeth. "Truly, you are an angel from heaven," continued Elizabeth.

"No, please, I'm just helping where I can," answered Wayne. "I can come back tomorrow and see if you're doing okay," he offered. "It's not necessary at all, but thank you very much," affirmed Elizabeth. "Can I get you anything to drink Wayne?" she asked. "If it's not too much trouble I would drink a glass of water," replied Wayne. "No trouble at all, really," said Elizabeth as she poured two glasses of water, one for each of them.

"So, how are you doing, Wayne? I haven't heard from you, of course, since before I left the community? Are you still helping with your family's farm? How is your mother? I always thought she was a lovely lady," acknowledged Elizabeth. "Thank you for asking, but I'm sorry to say that my mother passed away. She was always very ill when I was growing up," said Wayne. "Oh, I'm so terribly sorry. I didn't know. I feel awful," cried Elizabeth. "How could you have known? It's hard for me, but more so for my father. He's loved her since they were kids," acknowledged Wayne. "Now that it's just my father and me at the house there is also a lot of work to go around, but we manage alright," said Wayne. "I wish there was something I could do for you after all you have done for me," echoed Elizabeth.

"Just take care of yourself and your baby. I promise that I will come by the house when I can, even if you tell me not to. Only if you insist that I am not welcome, I will not come," said Wayne. "Well then, I guess, James and I wouldn't mind some company once in a while," she replied. "I apologize Ms. Elizabeth, but I have to meet my father for dinner. You won't mind if I leave, will you?" asked Wayne. "No, not at all," whispered Elizabeth, despite the fact that she was enjoying the company and a distraction from her heartache.

As Wayne excused himself and sauntered towards the door, Elizabeth followed him to the door to see him out, and Wayne extended his hand for a handshake, but Elizabeth decided a hug would be much more appropriate given the circumstance. Wayne's arms enclosed around Elizabeth like the wings of a dove, and she felt her spirit lifted by his warmth, his presence, and his support. Elizabeth found herself hugging him with an intensity that she did not expect, but she relished the embrace even after he had departed from her home. She found herself thinking about the hug from Wayne, but to the same extent she couldn't help but remember the feel of hugs from her husband. She was upset that she was starting to forget his smell. She had saved one of his favorite t-shirts, but his smell had long since disappeared from the shirt. Whilst the night folded around Elizabeth, baby James fell fast asleep in his new crib, and Elizabeth's eyed drooped and shut.

Chapter 7: From a Widow's Window

Despite Elizabeth's insistence that Wayne did not need to stop by the house on a daily basis, Wayne was true to his word, as a captain is to his crew during a storm at sea. Elizabeth had her own storm at sea, so to speak, and Wayne had slowly become her anchor. Elizabeth had never thought of Wayne in any other way than platonic before, but his frequent visits to the house gave her hope that James would have a semi-normal childhood. As she washed the dishes she caught herself looking out the window and watching Wayne hold little James. Her heart broke as she saw how good Wayne was with her baby, but she winced when she thought about how it should have been her husband holding James. She turned away quickly as she did not want the others to think additional bad things about her. As it was, the entire community seemed to be on edge with her decision to return to the community. Such a situation was completely unheard of, until her actually.

Even after turning away from the window she glanced again out the window at Wayne and James. Wayne reminded her oddly of her deceased husband, but only in a few ways. Elizabeth imagined that if her husband had been the chance to be a father to their baby he would have held little James the same way. Elizabeth couldn't seem to keep up with caring for James, herself, and the home, but Wayne was quite faithful in helping her. It seemed almost too nice. Who comes almost every day to care for a young widow, unless... thought Elizabeth... unless

Wayne had other interests. It finally occurred to her that Wayne maybe was interested in Elizabeth despite being a widow with a baby. Wayne saw her looking out the window at him. She waved innocently and quickly diverted her eyes back to her dishes, so she could pretend that she wasn't looking intentionally.

The problem was that Elizabeth felt torn emotionally in so many ways that she didn't know if she could be with someone else again ever. She didn't know if she should feel guilty for maybe even considering that she *MIGHT* like Wayne and that Wayne *MIGHT* like her. She felt *almost* like she did when she noticed that she had feelings for James after the first time they met. As guilt sunk in her smile turned upside down. Wayne re-entered the cottage shortly thereafter with baby James asleep in his arms. Although he could see something was wrong he didn't dare to ask what it was. He realized that they both were staring at each other through the window, but that probably was not a good topic of conversation.

"Well, can I help you with anything else? You sure look tired? I could watch James while you get some rest. He's asleep anyway. It's really no trouble at all Liz... Elizabeth. Sorry," stated Wayne. "You can call me Liz, it's not a problem. You don't have to be embarrassed. It's just, I'm amazed that you come here every day to help us. I'm certain that you have other people to care for, like yourself too, sometimes. Don't you think?" commented Elizabeth.

"Of course, but a good Amish man always respects an upstanding lady like yourself," replied Wayne. "If I didn't know any better, I'd think you were trying to charm me," said Elizabeth as she laughed and felt herself blush a little. "Well, maybe I am," Wayne said as he laughed a little before he continued, "I better be going then. I have to water the field. It's been hot these days and the crops just aren't growing like they should be." "Sure, good night then, and thank you, really," said Elizabeth. "Good night Liz," echoed Wayne as he walked away while a smile grew across his face.

Chapter 8: Baby Steps

The days passed for Wayne is a similar fashion. He worked the fields in the very early morning with his father. He prepared a light lunch for him and his father, took an afternoon siesta and then went to Liz's house around 3 pm every day, like clockwork. Wayne enjoyed his daily pattern but longed for something more with Liz. Although he didn't want to push her, especially considering that the two-year anniversary of her husband's death was approaching, he felt pulled towards her. Two years was more than one, but he knew very well that the heart healed only with time. Much as he felt with the passing of his own mother, he learned by day to grieve, but also to love, laugh, and smile again. Perhaps an even larger blessing than Liz or his father in his life was little baby James. Little baby James was not so little anymore and was growing into a healthy boy.

The first day that James took his first steps Wayne was at the house to watch him walk. While James walked to his mother, Elizabeth, who caught him and held him delicately in his arms, Wayne could not resist his own tears. Almost everything he could have dreamed of happening was already coming true. He didn't need to know everything, he didn't need to know the future with Liz and her son because in that moment everything was okay. In the face of everything they had passed together and separately, Elizabeth was coming to understand that everything he had done for her was not just out of respect, but also because he cared for her deeply.

Baby James turned with the help of his mother and started to take a few steps towards Wayne and uttered one syllable. Da. Wayne and Elizabeth could not have been happier or sadder as James grew and as they witnessed James walk and speak the word Da. In any case, Wayne was not James' biological father, but he was his father now, as much as his Elizabeth's husband was, if not more.

A few things were still missing from Elizabeth's life, including the acceptance of her parents and an understanding of what her relationship with Wayne was, but she stopped questioning it and accepted life as it was. She thought less about the English world, but she did occasionally receive visits from Meg, who wholeheartedly approved of Wayne, but did not yet utter it out loud. At least, in these moments, Elizabeth found peace, and her sense of self once more. She had an identity not just as a widow, but more importantly as a mother, a woman, and a friend. There were times, of course, that she still wondered what her life would be like if her husband had not passed away suddenly and unexpectedly, but she recognized that God was with her and would protect her always, and in a way, Wayne was the Holy Spirit, her dove, and little James, her son, symbolized Jesus Christ.

The stars were not always aligned in her favor, but a certain coffee-stained mug on her kitchen table was never empty to her. It was imperfect, but it was perfect to her. It was chipped on one side and the imperfectness of the mug was apparent to any stranger in her home, but to Elizabeth, the mug was like her home. The red lines across the center of the mug were slightly faded from use, and in her mind, the missing piece simply added character. Recently, a bright blue thumbprint had been added to the mug since James took a liking to paint. In spite of everything, life was whole, as whole as it could be, if you were a young Amish widow.

A Little Bit of Amish Faith

Alana Wilson

The streets were just beginning to get dark as Nicholas drove home. He can still hear his boss's, no, ex-boss's words echoing in the back of his mind, *I'm sorry Nicky, but we can't keep you employed if you have to call in every other day with a family emergency. It's just not how business works...* Nicholas felt himself grinding his teeth as he sped down the poorly lit backroad to his house. His headlights flashed across the wet asphalt as his mind wandered. *How am I going to tell my mom? How am I going to get groceries now and her medicine?* His mind ran circles. His headlights flashed across trees as his truck hit a patch of ice and skid. Nicholas turned the wheel hard and tried to correct the vehicle in time.

His headlights flashed across a figure that dove out of the way of his vehicle as it careened towards the ditch. Nicholas finally regained control and swerved hard. His truck skidded to a stop on the shoulder. Nicholas opened the door and slid out of the driver seat; adrenaline rushed through his body. He took shaky steps to the edge of the road. He peered down into the ditch, looking for the dark figure. They lay in the dirty snow. Nicholas slid down the bank to the figure's side. He saw in the pale twilight that it was a girl; she wore a thick dark coat over a plain dark blue dress and a starched white cap on her head. She groaned and sat up slowly.

"Are you okay?" Nicholas felt his heart pounding in his ears and his hands trembled.

"I, I think so." She replied quietly. He helped her to her feet and she groaned, leaning into him.

"I think I twisted my ankle," she said with a grimace.

"I'm so sorry. Let me take you to a doctor." Nicholas started to almost drag her up the ditch.

"Oh, no. That won't be necessary. I'm fine, really." She said shyly.

"Please let me take you to a doctor, or at least somewhere we can look at your ankle in the light." He looked at her pleadingly. He could almost see her debating it internally.

"I guess it wouldn't hurt to get it looked at, just in case it is serious," she said quietly. He sighed in relief. They scrambled up the bank to Nicholas's truck. He helped her into the passenger seat and scrambled around to his side.

"I'm so sorry, again. I didn't see you and the road was slick... I'm just so sorry." He trailed off as he looked at her face; she had a few minor scratches and scrapes.

"I forgive you. Everything happens for a reason; that is God's plan." She glanced out the window distantly.

"What are you even doing out here?" He tried to keep one eye on her and one eye on the road.

She was pretty, even in the dim light. Nicholas could see wisps of dark brown hair peeking out from under her cap and her dark green eyes were glassy. A light blush colored her cheeks. Nicolas caught a glimpse of his own nervous brown eyes in the mirror.

"I was walking back from the bakery in town. My uncle and aunt own it, and I work there whenever they need a hand. With the holidays around the corner, they're starting to get backed up with orders."

"You think they need any other help?" He chuckled nervously. She didn't respond. He drove the truck in silence. She held her hands clasped tightly in her lap.

"What's your name?" He finally said, breaking the tense silence.

"Naomi." She muttered.

"I'm Nicholas." He smiled at her.

He parked the truck outside the clinic in town. He helped Naomi out of the truck and inside. Doctor Schaffer sat at the front desk, working on paperwork; she was a middle aged woman, with streaks of gray coloring her ashy blonde hair and wrinkle just starting to appear at the corners of her eyes and mouth.

"Nicholas? Naomi? What are you two doing here so late at night? And together?" She said, and walked around the counter. Nicholas couldn't help but stare between the doctor and Naomi.

"Good evening, doctor. Nicholas here found me after I took a spill down the ditch outside town. I think I twisted my ankle." Naomi smiled sweetly up at the doctor. The doctor tutted and shook her head.

"Well, let's take you back and have a look at that ankle. Nicholas, would you mind giving me a hand here," Doctor Shaffer said, helping Naomi to her feet. Nicholas helped Naomi hobble to the exam room down the hall and onto the table.

"Well, I'll be on my way then. Will you be all right getting home, miss?" Nicholas edged towards the doorway.

"Nicolas, if you could take a seat in the waiting room, actually. I'll check on Naomi, and if it's too serious for my taste, I want you to drive her home so she doesn't overstrain herself." Doctor Shaffer smiled at Nicholas and ushered him out of the room. Nicolas wandered back to waiting room and slumped into a chair. He felt the weight of the day on his shoulders. *How could I be so stupid? I lose my job, I almost kill someone... I need to get my act together and fast,* he thought to himself. He rubbed his eyes and tried to shake the weariness.

Naomi hobbled down the hall on a crutch, back to the waiting Nicholas. He smiled shyly at her. Doctor Shaffer shuffled down the hall behind her.

"Okay, Naomi has a severe sprain and needs to stay off her ankle for a few weeks," Doctor Shaffer said, looking between the two.

"Thanks, Doc." Nicholas held open the door as Naomi hobbled outside. Nicholas helped her back into the truck. They drove down the road in silence.

"I'm sorry. Again."

"It all happened for a reason." Naomi looked out the passenger window thoughtfully.

Farms passed by as Nicholas drove down the back roads that led to the Amish community. He slowed down as the roads turned from asphalt to gravel. He stopped the truck at the gate of their community.

His headlights couldn't pierce the darkness that stretched further down the road.

"Do you need any help?" He turned to her. She looked at him, almost glared.

"No. I'll be just fine. I think you've done enough," she snarled at him and slammed the door open. She slid out of the truck and started to hobble down the dirt road. Nicholas followed her.

"Okay, I understand if you're upset. I messed up big time tonight, and you're nothing more than an innocent bystander. Please, let me try to make this right." He almost reached for her hand. Almost.

"No, this is far enough. I will be shunned by my community if they see me with you, especially in your vehicle. I can make it from here. Thank you for everything, but I hope we do not meet again in the future." She brushed an angry tear from her cheek and turned away from him.

"Let me walk with you, then. It's too dark and cold to be alone." She sighed heavily.

"Fine. But after tonight, I wish to never speak to you again," she glared at him and continued on her way.

"That's fair." Nicholas shrugged.

They walked down the dark country road in utter silence. Nicholas kept stealing glances at Naomi, trying to read her face. It occurred to him at that moment, this was the first time he had really forgotten about himself. He thought about her instead. *Is she married yet? I know the Amish girls get married young...* His thoughts wandered to who she was, what her life was like. He didn't think any more about his mother and brother waiting for him at home, or the heaviness in his heart from his father's recent passing, or the weariness in his joints from working all hours of the day.

She stopped at a tall white farm house. An old woman sat on the porch, reading by the light of a lantern. Nicholas stood at the bottom of the stairs as Naomi shuffled onto the porch. The old woman mumbled something at her. Naomi sighed and turned back to Nicholas. The old woman nodded and stood creakily.

"Nicholas, thank you for your assistance," she said quietly.

He opened his mouth to say something but she ducked inside before the words came out. Nicholas raised his hand in an awkward wave and walked back down the road. The darkness enveloped him, but for the first time in a long time, he felt clear headed. He walked in the chilly autumn night.

Nicholas sat in his truck outside his little two-story house. All the lights were off. The clock on the radio read 11:53. He trudged inside wearily. In the living room, his mother was asleep on the couch. His old lab, Gunner, greeted him at the front door with a small huff. Nicholas woke his mother up with a gentle shake.

"Mom, I'm home. Let's get to bed." He picked her up gently. She seemed to get smaller every day. He carried her down the hall and set her gently in bed. He pulled off her slippers and her fleece robe. She snuggled under the blankets with a soft sigh. He shut her door quietly behind him. Upstairs, he checked on his little brother Kevin. The fifteen-year-old boy lay deep asleep. Nicholas pulled his quilt back on him and walked down the hall to his own room. Nicholas collapsed into his bed, his shoes still on.

Nicholas woke early the next morning. His alarm blared loudly next to him. His crawled out of bed. Nicholas crept down the hall. The sun hadn't risen yet, and neither had anyone else in the house. He drove to town, trying to rub sleep from his eyes. He parked outside the diner in town and trudged inside.

He sat at the counter and drank a cup of black coffee. His phone screen glared back at him, reflecting the harsh facts of his life. *Bank account: $92.63. Mortgage due next Tuesday. Electricity bill due tomorrow.* He couldn't help but sigh heavily into his coffee. He still needed to pick up groceries and his mother's medication. As the sun finally peaked its head fully above the horizon, Nicholas walked down

Main Street. His eyes scanned the buildings looking for any 'help wanted' signs, but there were none to be seen.

But as he walked on, he did see something interesting; Naomi walking on her crutches down the other side street. Her face was red from exertion. He crossed the street at a jog and came to a stop in front of her.

"Morning," he croaked shyly.

"Hello," she growled and tried to move around him.

"Wait." He almost reached for. She stopped to listen, but didn't turn to look at him.

"I'm sorry, for last night. Do you need any help? The bakery is still a bit down the road and I'm sure it's taken you all morning to get to this point."

"And?" She snarled again.

"Let me give you a ride. Please. I want to make up for my actions," he pleaded. She was silent for a moment and then sighed.

"I guess I'm no use to my aunt if I show up at the end of the day."

"Great. Just wait here, I'll get my truck." Nicholas raced off to get his truck and pulled up next to Naomi.

They drove down the road quietly. The radio played a quiet news report, the only sound in the small cab of the truck. The bakery was just outside of town, a tourist trap. The building was squat, white-washed and impeccably clean. The parking lot was just a gravel lot. It smelled like fresh-baked bread and cinnamon rolls. He parked and helped her out of the truck.

"Well, I don't think I need any further assistance. Thank you, Nicholas." She shuffled into the bakery. Nicholas watched her go, feeling some small tug towards her. He let his feet carry his to the door and then inside. Naomi hobbled to the back on her crutches. A middle-aged woman, dressed in the same clothes as Naomi came out.

"Good morning, how can I help you?" She smiled politely at Nicholas.

"Oh, I was wondering if I could help you actually. I'm an acquaintance of Naomi's and I know she has a pretty bad sprain, so I was hoping I could help out until she's feeling better." He felt his cheeks burn. The woman studied him for a minute. She raised a finger to him and the disappeared into the back. He could hear the hushed voices as Naomi and the woman talked. The woman came back and looked Nicholas up and down.

"If you'd like to help, you are to be here from dawn to dusk. What is your work ethic like?"

"I'm willing to do anything. I can lift things and I'm good with tools and I can be here early or late or whatever you need." His heart raced. Naomi glared at him from the doorway.

"Alright then. You'll be paid every week, in cash of course. How does $300 a week sound? And this will be temporary, just until Naomi is back on her feet." The woman laughed now. Nicholas smiled.

"This is great. I can start right now. If you need me to." He felt giddy now.

"Ay, get back there and start moving those flour sacks from the back door to the pantry." He slid past the woman and almost tripped over Naomi's crutch.

Nicholas was satisfied in this new work. It was labor-intensive, which he didn't mind. But what he liked the most was picking up Naomi in the mornings. She had gotten permission from her community for Nicholas to pick her up at the gates and to drive her to work. They would talk sometimes early in the morning, about their favorite books, the weather, their families. He learned so much about her; she lived with her aunt and uncle, who owned the bakery she worked at, and her grandmother lived with them. She shared a room with her six cousins; four boys and two girls. She learned that he lived with his mother and younger brother. He had worked many job since dropping out of high school to take care of sick mother. He had played a game called lacrosse in school and he tried to explain the game to her on multiple occasions.

When they worked together, Nicholas couldn't help but look at Naomi from time to time. Her aunt had set up a stool at the front counter so she wouldn't have to stand all day. He would sometimes stare, and then catch himself and get back to work. He would chastise himself every time. But he couldn't help but notice how pretty she would look, like when she had smidges of flour smeared on her face or the smile she would use when her uncle told a joke while they sat in the kitchen baking loaf after loaf of bread. But she looked the nicest when they sat in his truck after work, when the sun came in the passenger window just right and caught a few stray hairs that had slipped out from under her cap during the day and made her cheeks look rosy and full. One day, after Nicholas had worked been driving her for a few weeks, Naomi looked at him curiously.

"I understand that you live with your mother and brother, but would you mind if I asked what happened to your father?"

"He didn't run off if that's what you're asking," Nicholas chuckled," He was, uh, killed a few months ago in a drunk driving accident. It's been rough on my mom and Kevin, but it's been getting better."

"I'm sorry to hear that. My parents passed when I was quite young. Also from an auto accident." She looked down at her hands soberly.

"That sucks. I'm sorry that happened to you. Doesn't God just have a sick sense of humor?" Nicholas wanted to punch himself in the face for opening his stupid mouth.

"God doesn't have a sense of humor. Everything He plans, it is for a reason." She replied calmly.

"Oh really? So God killed my dad and made my mother sick for some important reason," Nicholas snarled at her.

"Yes. What is your mother sick with?" She studied Nicholas's face.

"Cancer. It's terminal."

"I'm sorry. But did you think ever think God gives His hardest battles to His most worthy children?" She smiled at him.

"Why?" Nicholas stared straight ahead at the road.

"Because there will always be evil in the world and God must make sure He has soldiers to fight that evil, on earth and from heaven," she said, getting a powerful air behind her voice. Something intense, passionate.

"So, my mom and dad are soldiers for God?" Nicholas scoffed lightly.

"Most likely. If not, then they have a good place in heaven for them, something peaceful and rewarding." She smiled peacefully, as if thinking about what Heaven looks like.

"That's, that's actually really nice to think about. Thank you, Naomi." He noticed from the corner of his eye the small blush creeping up her neck.

Weeks passed and autumn turned into winter. Nicholas became a fixture at the bakery at the edge of town; something was always needing to be fixed and Naomi's cousins were a bit too young to be working there yet. He fixed ceiling tiles and the siding outside. He helped Naomi's uncle repair the window panes and learned how to make everything from a loaf of bread to the biggest wedding cake with pristine white frosting. He discovered he had a knack for frosting cupcakes and kneading dough. He continued to drive Naomi to the bakery and couldn't wait to see her every morning.

"Nicholas, I got you a present," she said one day, sliding a brown paper package across the seat to Nicholas as he picked her up one morning. He raised an eyebrow and opened the present. Inside, a long navy scarf sat folded neatly. He pulled it on and almost blushed; it smelled like Naomi.

"Thank you, this is wonderful Naomi." The thick scarf was warm and soft on his neck.

"Oh, I just thought you could use something warm, since it's cold out and you don't really wear anything besides that jacket," she trailed off as her red nose was matched with a red blush. He reached over and took her hand, looking her in the eye.

"Seriously, thank you, Naomi." She blushed harder and looked away. Nicholas still caught the little smile that stayed on her face for the rest of the day.

Nicholas looked through the window at the jewelry sitting on the velvet display. Everything was going good; the bills were all paid, he had presents for his mother and brother for Christmas. But something was missing. Silver watches and gold chains sat on the black cloth, glittering at him. *I can't afford any of these thing... She probably wouldn't even like it...* He had never seen Naomi wear anything other than her plain dresses and stark white cap. She wore thick gloves and a heavy coat now that it was winter, but she didn't wear makeup or jewelry. He wracked his brain trying to think of something she would actually like.

He walked down the street. It was Sunday night, the only day he got off from the bakery. They were going to close a few days before Christmas and a few days after to celebrate with their community, so Nicholas wanted to get something for Naomi before the holiday. His thoughts wandered as the snow began to fall in thick flakes. He wasn't paying attention and bumped into a girl walking the opposite direction; he knocked the bags from her hands.

"Oh, jeez. I'm so sorry. I didn't mean to." He started to pick up her bags.

"You said that when we first met." She said. Nicholas looked up at her and froze. Naomi stood there, wearing her hair down in soft curls and a cute sweater dress. She wore some makeup, just enough to highlight but not overpower.

"Naomi," he muttered.

"Surprise," she said softly.

"What are you doing here? Don't you need to," he trailed off as he took her in completely.

"I just needed to come into town, and it feels better to look like an English, to blend in better. I saw you from across the street and thought I might surprise you." She smiled and took her bags from him.

"This is a surprise. I was just doing some shopping myself." He blushed slightly.

"Well, then would you mind escorting me home. I like to walk on nights like this when the air is crisp and you can see the stars so clearly." She took his arm and they walked down the street.

They walked quietly for a long time. She grasped his hand firmly; her cold fingers felt so tiny in his. He held her bags in his other hand, like a gentleman. Their breaths billowed in tiny clouds. Cars didn't pass by them in the quiet night. The only sound was their feet crunching through the snow.

"So what did you need to buy," he joked.

"Just a few things from the hardware store. My uncle ran out of nails and he wants to finish up some presents for my cousins so I ran out to get some."

"You're so sweet," he chuckled and squeezed her hand gently.

"So what were you doing in town so late," she teased back.

"Just looking for a present," he shrugged. "For my mom," he added quickly.

"That's very sweet of you, Nicholas. So what were you thinking of getting her?"

"Oh, I can't decide. I wanted to get something nice and fancy for her, but also something practical like a sweater. She does like sweaters. Or a new pair of slippers, ones with thick lining." He had already bought her a thick sweater and a pair of slippers that looked like cats, because she liked silly things like that.

"How about some thick socks?" Nicholas laughed hard at her. "Oh, I know, socks! How exciting! But she's sick, so some thick socks would be nice in case her toes are cold," she chuckled softly.

"That's a really good idea, actually. Thank you." He wanted to kiss her. But he didn't. They were friends, co-workers. He didn't want to impose on her beliefs either. He knew that the Amish were conservative and he didn't want to make her uncomfortable. They stopped outside the gates.

"I'll see you tomorrow." She looked up at him, and he swore she batted her eyelashes at him.

"Yeah. Tomorrow. Good night, Naomi." He smiled back as her fingers slipped from his and she took her bag back.

"Good night, Nicholas." She waved at him and walked down the lane.

Nicholas woke early the next morning. His present for Naomi sat on his desk. He grabbed his jacket and crept down the hall, the present tucked under his arm. He snuck to his mother's door and peaked in. She lay there, sleeping peacefully, a small smile on her face. He crossed the room to wake her up. He shook her arm gently. She was cold. He crossed the room and left. On the front porch, he pulled out his phone.

"Hello? Hi, yes, I need an ambulance. I think my mom is dead," he said blankly.

Nicholas sat on the front porch with Kevin. The flashing lights were blindingly bright. An officer squeezed Nicholas's shoulder and gave him a pitiful look. Kevin looked blankly ahead with red rimmed eyes. The paramedic walked down the stairs and stood in front of the boys. She smiled weakly at them.

"I'm sorry boys. Your mom was a good lady. I hear she was a great teacher. She passed in her sleep, so it was painless. She's in a better place now." Nicholas wanted to believe her but he just felt so angry.

After everyone left, it was deathly quiet. Nicholas called into the high school so Kevin wouldn't have to go in. Kevin sat on the couch, wrapped in their mother's favorite blanket. Nicholas didn't know what to say to him. He didn't have any words. *What kind of God orphans a boy?* Nicholas walked down the road aimlessly.

He found himself en route to the bakery and couldn't stop himself. *They would want to know why he was late.* He walked into the warm bakery and saw Naomi's aunt at the counter.

"Nicholas? Are you all right?" She walked around the counter nervously.

"Yeah, I'm fine. My mom died last night," he croaked.

"Oh Nicholas." She hugged him gently. Tears welled in his eyes. Naomi came from the back at that moment.

"Nicholas?" She wiped her hands on rag. He sniffled and left quickly. Outside, in the cold air, tears burned down his face. He heard the down shut behind him and someone grab his hand. He sniffled and wiped the tears roughly from his face.

"Nicholas? I thought you were hurt when you didn't show up this morning." Naomi sounded worried.

"I'm okay. My mom died last night. "He shivered from the cold. He turned to look at her.

"I'm so sorry, Nicholas," she said softly. He took her hands gently.

"Why? Why did she have to die?" He sobbed. Naomi hugged him tightly.

"It's God's will. She's in a better place." She muttered against his coat.

"But why? It's cruel! My brother is orphaned now! We're all alone now. Why would God do that to us?" He cried into her shoulder. She was much shorter than him, but he still held her tightly.

"I don't know, Nicholas. I'm sorry, but I don't have all the answers. Maybe He didn't want her to suffer any longer. And your brother has you. You have each other. You can always build a bigger family." She shushed him and rubbed his back soothingly.

"I don't know what to do any more, Naomi." He rubbed away the tears again.

"Just make it through today. Then make it through tomorrow. And that you aren't alone in this. You have people who will help you." She smiled sweetly up at him. He managed a weak smile back.

"Thank you." He said softly.

"Nicholas, I'm going to go back inside now. It's freezing out here!" She giggled and led him back inside the bakery.

Nicholas sat in the bakery that day, just watching. Naomi's aunt wouldn't let him work, so instead she made him drink hot tea and taste-test pastries. He felt empty inside. But he felt better knowing that Naomi was his friend, at least. She kept glancing at him throughout the day; when she caught his she offered only a smile.

"Nicholas, would you like to walk home with me?" Naomi pulled on her coat tightly as the sun dipped below the horizon.

"Oh, sure." He followed her out the door quietly.

The streets of the town were lit with bright Christmas lights. Nicholas felt tired. He hadn't felt this tired since he had first met Naomi. She took his hand as they walked. He shoved his hand in his other pocket, and felt her present, long forgotten from this morning. He blushed, thinking about how much he had wanted to give it to her in his truck this morning.

"Naomi, I know this is a bad time, but I got you a present. I know I'm not going to see you for like a week, so I wanted to get you something before the holiday. I was going to give it to you this morning but you know..." he trailed off. He took the present out and handed it to Naomi. She smiled up at him.

"Thank you, Nicholas. I know this must be hard." She ripped off the bright red wrapping paper and shoved it in her pocket. She opened the box carefully. Inside, nestled in white tissue paper was a book. It was an old Nancy Drew book of his mother's. He had asked her last night when he got home if he could give it to Naomi.

"I know you said you hadn't read anything good in a long time and my mom had this one lying around. I figured you might like something to read over the holiday and just enjoy." He blushed fiercely under the streetlights.

"Oh, Nicholas. That's so thoughtful. Thank you." She said and kissed his cheek gently. She stowed the book in her own pocket and they walked on. Her fingers laced through his. He felt his heart beating against his rib cage. At the edge of the Amish community, Naomi looked up at him. The night was quiet, peaceful.

"Nicholas, what are we doing," she whispered.

"I don't know. But it's working, isn't it?" He looked deep into her eyes.

"Is it? To be friends is one thing, but to be something more."

"Naomi, let's talk about this later, okay? Let's just be with our families now," he said back tensely.

"You're right. I'm sorry. Go and be with your brother. If you need anything, let me know. Please." She squeezed his hand and turned away from him.

"Thank you, Naomi. For everything," he called to her as she walked down the lane. She looked back over her shoulder and smiled sweetly at him.

At home, Nicholas found his brother asleep on the couch. He slumped against the doorway and rubbed his face. Christmas was just around the corner and it was going to be lonely. Their mother had been the one who set up the Christmas tree and always made them a big breakfast on Christmas morning. He couldn't imagine how empty the couch was going to look on Christmas morning, without their mother sitting there. He woke Kevin up and ushered him to bed. Nicholas collapsed into his own bed, wishing someone were there to hold him. Someone small, with wavy chocolate brown and deep green eyes.

Christmas morning was bleak. Kevin sat glaring at the stack of presents that were for their mother. Nicholas couldn't bear to open the present from his mother. Kevin locked himself in his room. Nicholas opened his mother's presents and cried. Kevin had gotten her a new travel book, for Mongolia. Nicholas stared blankly at the cozy slippers he had bought. Nicholas sat on the porch and read that travel book. He wished he was far away too. He wished he was happy again, wished his brother could be happy again. He wished Naomi was by his side. He wished he had her faith and grace. He looked up as Kevin sat down next to him.

"Hey, Nick."

"How you holding up, buddy?" He closed the book absentmindedly.

"I'm..." He shrugged.

"I'm sorry we can't have a big Christmas dinner or something. Something to make it all..." Nicholas couldn't find the words.

"It's fine. I understand, dude." They sat in silence for a while. The sun began to dip and the snow began falling. Kevin finally stood and went inside. Nicholas sighed. He stood to go inside when he heard someone coming up the gravel driveway. Naomi stood at the bottom of his stairs, holding a basket. She wore her English sweater dress and leggings. A knit hat kept her wavy hair in check.

"Merry Christmas, Nicholas." She said softly.

"Merry Christmas, Naomi. What are you doing here?" Nicholas helped her up the stairs.

"Helping the less fortunate," she teased," Are you going to invite me in? I've got a big dinner that I need to get started."

"Of course, come in." Nicholas was dazed. He took her coat and led her into the kitchen. She smiled sweetly at him as she started cooking. Kevin glanced at him from the stairs.

"You want to come down and meet Naomi? She knows I can't cook and came to make sure you didn't die of starvation," he joked. Kevin shrugged and shuffled down the stairs. Nicholas led him into the kitchen.

"Naomi? Sorry to interrupt, but this is my brother, Kevin. Kevin, this is my friend, Naomi." Naomi smiled and offered her hand. Kevin shook it weakly. Kevin turned to Nicholas.

"She's pretty," he remarked and trudged into living room.

"He seems to be doing okay." She turned back to the cutting board.

"Yeah. He's just jealous he can't snag a nice girl like you," he flirted and then blushed heavily. Naomi blushed slightly too.

"So, how have you been?" She didn't look up from the vegetables she was cutting.

"It's been rough. It's nice to see you, though. I've kind of missed seeing you every day." He pulled a soda out of the fridge and hopped up onto the counter next to her.

"I've missed talking to you, too, Nicholas. It's been quiet. Food will be done in about forty-five minutes." She smiled at him, and Nicholas swore his heart skipped a beat. She looked so natural in his kitchen.

"I finished that book you gave me. And the note inside was sweet." She glanced at him.

"Note?" He raised an eyebrow.

"From your mother? She just said that she was glad I was your friend and that she couldn't be more thankful that somebody had gotten you out of your shell."

"Oh, I didn't know she wrote that. That's so like her." He muttered. He couldn't help but smile at the thought of his mother always looking out for him.

"She must've been quite a woman to have raised you and your brother."

"She was. I miss her." He sipped his soda pensively. Naomi placed her hand on his knee gently. He grasped it and gave her fingers a gentle squeeze.

"Why don't you set the table? It'll only take a few more moments." She smiled gently at him.

They sat around the dinner table. The silence was almost palpable. Kevin poked at the carrots and potatoes on his plate. Nicholas kept stealing glances at Naomi. Naomi didn't take her eyes off her plate either. Nicholas cleared his throat loudly.

"Kevin, what do you think?" Nicholas fixed his younger brother with a hard stare.

"It's good. Thank you, Naomi." He mumbled into his roast potatoes. Nicholas kicked him under the table.

"So, what are you learning in school, Kevin? I didn't get to go to high school," Naomi asked.

"Evolution." Kevin snarled. He stood and left the table.

"Kevin!" Nicholas stood and shouted at him.

"It's okay, Nicholas. He's just feeling hurt. Let him be, he'll come around." Naomi squeezed his hand. Nicholas sat slowly and looked at her. His heart sped up as she battered her lashes slowly at him.

"What are you saying, Naomi?" He felt her small hand in his; it felt like it was two halves made whole.

"Well, if you'll have me, I'd like to stay." She stared at his hands.

"On one condition," he whispered.

"Yes?" She looked deep into his eyes. He could stare at her eyes for forever.

"Kiss me. Please." She smiled and leaned forward slightly. He closed the gap between them and pressed his lips against hers. Time seemed to stop in that second; he was aware of only her in the room. He kept his hands firmly on the table, afraid of startling her like a deer. She leaned back slowly.

"I should go talk to Kevin," Nicholas breathed. His heart still pounded against his chest.

"I'll be right here," she giggled. And unspoken, *I'll be waiting*, hung between them.

Nicholas climbed the stairs and almost ran down the hall to Kevin's room. He knocked loudly. No response. He cracked the door to find Kevin sitting on his bed. Kevin didn't look at him.

"Hey buddy."

"So, your girlfriend is going to be my new mom?" Kevin said blankly. Nicholas sat on the edge of Kevin's bed and sighed.

"No, not at all. She's just here because, I guess, she loves me. She knows what it's like to lose her parents. She's not going to be your new mom or anything more than my girlfriend. But she's going to have a rough time adjusting to this role."

"What?" Kevin looked at Nicholas like Nicholas had grown a second head.

"She's Amish. She's not quite up to date with all the relationship standards of us regular people," he chuckled.

"So?"

"So just come downstairs and give her a chance. Eat something besides a pop tart or ramen. I mean, she did cook us actual food."

"Okay, but just dinner. I'm not sticking around for dessert." Kevin trudged to the door and down the stairs.

As they sat around the table again, Nicholas felt a weight fall off his shoulders, a weight he forgot he was carrying. Nicholas saw his future at that dinner table, and he liked what he saw. He was at peace, at last.

MELISSA

Melissa

The weather seemed to mimic her sentiments as the rain splattered relentlessly down her shirt and slithered through her pant legs, to her shoes, creating a sloshing puddle in the base of the worn soles. Well, the holes don't seem like such a big deal now, do they? She thought to herself, bemused. She tried to adjust the umbrella but there was no angle that the wind wasn't sending the rain so the effort was an exercise in futility. She cocked her head to the side and peered down the street again to see if the bus was approaching but she could not see much through the spattering on her cheeks. Sighing she retreated into the already crammed bus shelter. The bus was late and that was nothing new but the grumbling within the glass enclosure was almost too much for Melissa to bear in her current state. She almost went back out to stand in the storm to avoid listening to the commuters irritated complaints. Every day after work it was the same twenty people making the same inane conversations about the weather and politics and how the bus was inevitably late. Usually Melissa welcomed the idle chatter as a distraction to her own woes but today she was overwhelmed with depression. She reached into her enormous handbag and retrieved her cell phone. She peered at it hopefully but of course it was still out of service. The bill hadn't been paid in three months. It was probably for the best – Michelle's divorce was about to be finalized and Melissa wasn't sure she had the internal strength to listen to any more of her sister's tears. She was immediately ashamed by her thought. Michelle was having a terrible time. This marriage had only lasted six months. Melissa didn't understand how Michelle kept tying the knot when her unions always seemed to fail so miserably. Some people just can't be alone. I hope I am not one of those people. Dear God, please let mine and Greg's marriage last forever. Again, she was flooded with guilt. Of course, they would last forever. They had been together since infancy, grown up together two houses apart. Greg had adored her for as long as she could remember and she, him. Yet Melissa couldn't help but feel that there had been a shadow cast upon them since their engagement last spring. Almost as soon as he had proposed, things had gone from bad to worse. Melissa's mother had been diagnosed with terminal breast cancer and died three months later. Melissa's biological father had appeared after a ten-year absence but only because he thought he could somehow capitalize on her mother's passing. When that didn't pan out for him, he skipped town once more. Michelle had just finalized her second divorce at that time. Then Greg lost his job at the factory and was picking up odd jobs wherever he could find them. The only constant had been Melissa. Melissa and her meager paying waitressing gig at the truck stop. She managed to keep paying the property taxes on the house after her mom went to heaven and she helped maintain the payments on Greg's truck so he could still go job hunting and work jobs when he got them but money was beyond tight and the wedding date was approaching faster than she had anticipated. I should ask Greg about changing the date. But some little nagging voice in her head told her if she did that, the date would never occur at all. Before she could chastise her subconscious for such an appalling notion, the bus flew up unexpectedly, drenching her further. Sighing, she boarded the bus, swishing, and squeaking. The vehicle was filled to capacity and Melissa was standing wedged between an old Asian man who smelled quite like a summer meadow and a seated middle-aged woman. She looked apologetically at the woman as droplets of water dripped off her shabby coat and onto the lady. The woman looked up at Melissa with luminous gray eyes and smiled in a way that actually warmed her right to the core of her heavy heart. For one brief second, Melissa felt content. Then a confusion set it.

"I'm sorry, ma'am. The rain..." Melissa trailed off. The woman continued to smile at her but said nothing. She merely shook her head and shrugged. Melissa was overcome by a strange sense of de ja vu.

"Ma'am, do I know you?" she asked timidly. It always sounded so cliché when people asked that question. The lady's smile widened but she shook her head again.

"I don't think so, child," she replied. Her voice was a light, throaty whisper. "But God bless you." Then she stood up but before she shuffled away toward the exit, she reached up, touched the gold cross which hung around her neck and stroked Melissa's cheek. The chain and pendant had belonged to her mother.

"Remember, child, the darkest hour is just before the dawn." And then she was gone.

Melissa literally had to wring out her clothes once she walked into the safety of her house. The storm seemed to have worsened over the hour and a half it had taken her to get home. She was freezing and sniffling and just before she could jump into the welcoming warmth of the newly filled bathtub, the doorbell rang. For a brief moment, looking at the almost steaming water in her peripheral vision, she contemplated ignoring the caller but she was fairly certain it was either Greg or Michelle. With that realization, the urge to ignore grew stronger. Alas, Melissa was not the girl to turn her back on her family; no matter how much they deserved it.

She threw on a pair of pajamas and hurried down the rickety stairs to the front door. Greg pushed his way into the house, already soaked to his skin.

"Sorry," he apologized as he rushed for shelter, pooling water all over the fading carpet. "That storm is really something else!"

Melissa nodded her agreement and after shutting the door joined her fiancé in the living room.

"I would have called you today but my phone got cut off," she told him after giving him a brief hug and kiss. Greg looked guiltily at the floor.

"I know. I tried calling you too. I'm so sorry about that, Mel. Things will turn around soon. I worked today on a construction crew and they seemed to like me. I'm going back tomorrow too."

"Tomorrow? We're supposed to go looking for wedding venues tomorrow. It's my only day off this week, Greg."

"I know, Mel but we need the money. Listen, I was thinking about something..." Melissa looked at him expectantly. Then she shook her head when she saw the look in his eye. She already knew what he was going to say. This was probably the biggest problem with their relationship; even their thoughts were not sacred because they had known each other for so long a time.

"No. We've talked about this and the answer is still no, Greg."

"Oh come on, Mel. I can barely afford my car and you certainly can't afford this place by yourself. We should move in together and save some money for the wedding."

"No. This is my mom's house and she wouldn't have wanted us living together in it before we were married. No. End of discussion." Greg grunted and threw his hands up.

"Well at this rate, we're going to have to elope then." Melissa glared at him. He knew how important this wedding was to her. Everyone in her family had either eloped, divorced or gotten married at City Hall. There had not been one real ceremony in her immediate family, even with Michelle's three unions. Melissa desperately wanted to start her life with her husband properly, building a solid foundation from the get-go. Suddenly, she had an appalling thought. Maybe he's not the husband I'm supposed to build with.

Irene

I should have stayed home and taken that bath I never got, Melissa thought with some bitterness as she pushed her way through the marketplace. The rain had slowed to a miserable drizzle now, the sky lighter but still as gray and glum as Melissa was feeling. She didn't know what was wrong with her lately. It was so unlike her to be in such a grumpy place emotionally but she simply couldn't seem to shake the sense of doom which was stalking her. That morning when she had woken, she was determined to make the most of her day off so she forced a smile on her face and headed outside to face the world. And slowly, the rain and the late bus and the crowds chipped away at that fake beam until she was in the middle of the market, sulking again. She made her way into the center of the hub, not really sure what she was doing there. There were flowers to be bought, a band to be booked, food to be arranged but Melissa had only been thinking of the dress. Money had been so tight, she had taken to rummaging through her closet, looking for pieces of clothing she could possibly fashion into a wedding gown. Her mother's beautiful lace and satin piece had been horribly water damaged in the flood of '97 and Melissa had cried when she removed it, decaying from a trunk in the attic. Her dream had always been to wear it walking down the aisle with her father. She had a daydream where her father would turn to her on that magical day, look her in the eye and whisper, "You look just like your mother." But now that dream was shattered too. Who was she kidding? Her dad wouldn't walk her down the aisle unless she paid him. Ten years prior, he had made a startling announcement to his wife, Melissa's mother. He had fallen in love with Aunt Cathleen and they were moving to Mexico. No one had been more stunned than Melissa by the news. She had always idolized her father and her mother's sister had always been her favorite aunt. Now, in one fell swoop, both of them were gone. And gone they were. No one heard a word from them until four years later, when he called drunk, single and begging his daughters for money. Aunt Cathleen had left him for a much younger man and thrown him out of their houseboat in Mexico. Of course, neither Michelle nor Melissa were in a place to help him financially but somehow, the siblings had managed to procure a loan through a ridiculously high-interest rate through an independent company and gave him five thousand dollars. He vowed "to the good Lord Jesus above" that he would make every payment but by the time the first installment was due, his phone had been disconnected and no one heard from him again until their mother had passed. Michelle had put the loan on her bankruptcy but Melissa's credit was still ruined from her end. Yet it wasn't the money that scarred them. It was the betrayal by a man they had once loved so dearly.

Melissa angrily brushed a tear away from her face and suddenly stopped to look around. She was in an unfamiliar part of the market. This must be new. I've never seen this side before. As she looked over her shoulder, trying to orient herself, she heard a weak voice to her left.

"Are you lost, child?" Melissa turned to address the speaker. An ancient figure sat in a scarce booth, peering at her intently with large, inquisitive eyes. Melissa shook her head at the elderly woman and tried to smile but failed terribly. Suddenly, she felt overwhelmed by grief and loss. The woman was at her side in a nimble fashion one would not expect from someone so old. She patted her shoulder comfortingly.

"Come sit with me, child," the woman murmured, leading her behind the booth. "Why don't you tell me about it. I always find when I speak my worries aloud, they don't seem so cumbersome." Melissa swallowed the lump in her throat and sat on a wooden stool with the woman. She forced a small grin through her misty eyes.

"I'm sorry, ma'am. I...I'm supposed to be getting married soon...and I just don't know if I'm ready." Melissa's smiled broadened as she heard the lameness of her words but the lady just nodded sympathetically. Her shining green eyes shifted to the gold cross around Melissa's neck and she leaned forward, gently touching Melissa's golden crown of hair with a gnarled, arthritic hand.

"Have you a dress yet?"

Without warning, Melissa burst into a sea of tears as she shook her head.

"I can't afford a dress!" she moaned. "I can barely afford to eat! I don't know how we're going to have a wedding! I don't know if I should even be marrying him. Oh!"

Mortified, she jumped to her feet. "I am so terribly sorry! I don't know what came over me!"

The woman calmly placed her hands on Melissa's shoulders and sat her down on the stool again.

"You needed to get it out, child. An old woman's ears are the best place to do such things. Sometimes we even have solutions." For the first time, the old woman smiled and it was a gruesome sight. She was missing all but two of her teeth, one in the far bottom and one in the top front. Melissa cringed slightly and was instantly contrite. This person was showing her kindness in a time when she felt so incredibly alone.

When she was confident Melissa was not about to move again, the old timer shuffled to the side and Melissa was staring at an absolutely stunning wedding gown on a hanger. It was reminiscent of another era but which one, Melissa could not pinpoint. It had all of the elegance of the early 1920s with the flair of the 30's and 40's. It was a compilation of lace, crinoline and satin in a modest but stylish way. Melissa was in awe of its beauty, almost to the point of entrancement. She forced her eyes away but couldn't help but peer at it from the corner of her eye. It wasn't until much later that she realized it was also the only item in the booth.

"Do you like this dress, child?" Melissa nodded without raising her eyes. "It is very special and priceless with an incredible history."

"Was it yours?" Melissa asked politely, still fixated on the garment. The woman laughed.

"Heavens no. I am merely a vessel for the dress. She belongs to no one but sometimes she leads me to someone who needs her." Melissa was beginning to feel her irritability return. Great. The lady is loony.

She rose to her feet again.

"Well, it's lovely. I hope whomever she leads you to enjoys her very much." As she turned to leave, the woman began to cackle.

"The dress has chosen you, child. I thought you understood that." Melissa turned back, her brow furrowed.

"I just explained that I cannot afford this dress," she almost snapped. Crazy old bird.

"You don't need money for this but you do need to make a promise," the woman told her. Melissa paused. She was torn between wanting the intricate white creation before her and walking away from the unbalanced dame who was still speaking. Just promise her whatever she wants and run like the wind.

"Okay. I'll make a promise," Melissa finally agreed. "What is it?"

"You must promise to marry your betrothed and live out your marriage as God intended." Melissa blinked and tore her eyes away from the dress which had held her completely captive.

"Is that it?" she asked. The woman nodded.

"I promise to marry Greg and live out my marriage according to God's plan," Melissa repeated solemnly. She felt her heart skip a beat and for a split second, she was overcome by a heady, intoxicated feeling. Nodding, the older lady removed the dress from the hanger and gently wrapped it in a plastic garment bag before handing it to Melissa. Then she handed her a worn, leather-bound book.

"This comes with the dress," she told her. Then, as quickly as she had invited her into the booth, the woman was ushering her out.

"Go and live your life, child."

"Wait! What's your name?"

"You may call me Irene."

Alexandra

Melissa could not believe her good fortune. She hurried home in order to bring her precious gift to the shelter. Once inside the house, shaking off the rain, she couldn't help but wonder if she had just taken advantage of an elderly woman who had taken leave of her senses. In fact, the more Melissa thought about it, the more she realized that she had done a very foolish and possibly cruel thing. Tomorrow before work, I will go and return the dress. The old lady is probably suffering from dementia. That familiar disheartened feeling started to wash over her as she sat down on the plaid sofa and pulled off her rain boots. She shook her short blonde hair free of water droplets and stared blankly at the fireplace. I miss you, mama. I wish you were here. On impulse, Melissa threw two logs into the fireplace and lit it. Her mother used to love sitting by the fire. She would watch it for hours, lost in thought. Melissa and Michelle used to tease her about her fascination with the flames. Feeling an intense desire to be near her mom, Melissa tried to lose herself in the sparks also but she could not relax. Her head was too full to embrace a meditative state. She glanced around the room and her eyes rested on the book the old lady had bequeathed to her. Leaning forward, she picked it up. It appeared to be a journal of sorts but not written in the "Dear Diary" style. Melissa flipped to the first page. The inscription read, Alexandra, 1948.

May 4

Andrew proposed today. I suppose I should have been more excited but I was put off by his entire family being present. Where is the romance? Is our whole marriage going to be littered with his family? I don't know if I can marry a man who spends so much time with his relatives. I said "yes" but I have the sense that this engagement won't reach its fruition. He wants us to marry in the autumn.

May 9

We are barely betrothed and my future mother-in-law has already dominated the wedding plans. She insists that we have the ceremony at the Golf Club but I always wanted to marry on the beach. Andrew says I should simply let her have her way since he is her only child and she won't have an opportunity to help plan anyone else's wedding. I suppose I have no choice but to relent.

May 26

We are set to be married at the Golf Club on October 30th. Andrew's cousin Camila will be my maid of honor even though I desperately wanted my best friend Hazel to hold the title. I am quickly learning that Andrew's family always wins in these situations. I should call an end to this once and for all.

June 23

Why can't this family mind their own affairs? I feel like I can't breathe! I am constantly explaining myself to Andrew's mother on one subject or another. I don't know how much more I can take of this!

July 6

Andrew and I had a terrible argument today. He called me "cold" because I voiced my displeasure of his family's involvement in every aspect of our lives. I returned his engagement ring. I think it is best that we part ways. My heart is broken.

Unexpectedly, Melissa felt her eyes mist up. So he's close to his family. What's wrong with that? I wish that Greg were closer to his! As if on cue, there was a knock at the door. It was Greg, once again drenched from the storm. He bustled inside, shivering. He gave Melissa a peck on the cheek and smiled at her, boyishly. She was inexplicably annoyed with him.

"Why are you so late?" she demanded, glancing at the grandfather clock in the corner of the room. Greg's smile faltered and he shrugged nonchalantly.

"The job took longer than we thought. We still have more to do tomorrow." Melissa didn't reply but pursed her lips into a thin line. She suddenly understood exactly how Alexandra felt. He doesn't understand what's important to me. He's not the right man for me.

"Mel? I'm sorry about today. I know you wanted to go look at places for the wedding. But I have a feeling that this will lead to full-time employment."

"You have a feeling?" she snarled. She had no idea what had come over her. She was picking a fight but for reasons she could not comprehend. Greg looked completely perplexed by her tone.

"What's wrong?"

"Nothing. I'm just tired. It's late and I have to work tomorrow." She looked pointedly at the door. Greg turned red with humiliation.

"Are you telling me to go?" he asked incredulously. She had never thrown him out in their entire relationship. She nodded. Locking his jaw, Greg spun on his heel and headed back to the door.

"I'm doing this for us, Melissa. So you can have that all important wedding you need to have. You don't need to be so hostile." He did not wait for her reply before disappearing into the night. Sighing, she tossed another piece of firewood into the flames and plopped back down onto the sofa. She picked up the journal and continued to read.

July 30

I haven't seen or spoken to Andrew in three weeks. My heart does not want to mend. Imagine my surprise when his mother called on me this morning. I invited her in for tea. She told me that once, she had been just like me, a free spirit with an independent streak that would not be tamed. She had been shunned her own family when she had developed polio and it wasn't until Andrew's father began courting her did she understand what having people who cared about her was truly like. Soon, she had been adopted by their family and in turn, she had grown a close-knit family of her own. She told me that nothing was more important than family and sometimes, in order to keep that spirit alive, she would infringe too much in the lives of those she cared about. She apologized to me and then gave me an offering of peace; a handmade lace and satin wedding gown. She told me that it was rich in history and there was a mystery which surrounded it as it only sought out those who needed it. I couldn't stop staring at it as if I were under a spell. But she warned me that it could only be worn if I promised to live out my life with Andrew according to God's will and follow his guidance always. As I stared at that garment, all of my doubts about marrying Andrew disappeared. I agreed and embraced his mother.

Strangely, that was the final entry in the entire book, despite the fact that there were dozens more blank, browning pages within the leather binding. As Melissa flipped through the empty paper, a single business card slipped out. It read "Alexandra's Antiques" and there was a local address and phone number. Intrigued, Melissa picked up the home phone and called. The ringing was finally answered by a voice recording which stated the store's hours. Melissa slowly replaced the receiver. I'll have to go there one day and meet Alexandra.

Melissa woke at dawn the following morning and carefully wrapped the wedding dress into another plastic bag and then placed it in a brown paper bag along with the diary. She got dressed for work and headed out to the market. The cursed rain had yet to cease. It had been three days of gray, depressing weather. Regardless, she vowed to return the dress to Irene. She didn't feel right having taken it from such an obviously feeble-minded woman. Yet on the bus ride, she re-read the passage where Alexandra's mother-in-law to be explains the importance of the ceremonial attire. She had verbatim said what Irene had said. Oh pshaw. Irene probably wrote the journal herself.

As Melissa disembarked the bus, she looked around, attempting to recall where Irene's booth had been. She remembered it was in an obscure spot she had never seen before but after an hour of wandering the marketplace, she was unable to locate the old woman and her stand. In fact, she couldn't even find the area she had stumbled upon the previous day. Feeling guilty, Melissa returned to the bus stop. As she waited for the line which would take her to work, she suddenly realized that she was mere blocks from the spot where Alexandra's Antique's was located. On a whim, she decided to visit the store.

It took her less than ten minutes to get there and when she arrived, she was pleasantly surprised by a small, old brick structure displaying antique toys and relics from all walks of life. She opened the door, a chime announcing her arrival and hurried inside. As her eyes adjusted to the dimness of the store, she eagerly looked at the counter, completely expecting Irene to be there. To her disappointment, a young man, just barely out of his teens was leaning over the counter, playing on his laptop. He completely ruined the old fashioned energy which had embraced her. Sullenly, Melissa turned to leave but the man-boy called out.

"May I help you, miss?" His polite demeanor surprised her. She paused and turned back to him.

"No...I...well maybe. Is this Alexandra's Antiques?" she asked, feeling witless as the words left her lips. The young man smiled welcomingly.

"Yes. Can I help you find something?"

"No...I...well...I'm looking for Alexandra." The boy's smile faltered.

"I'm sorry, miss. My mom is quite ill and in the hospital. Are you a friend?" Melissa was aghast at her own stupidity. Of course, the Alexandra from the book could not have been his mother. The boy was much too young. It was merely a coincidence that the store was named the same name. Melissa shook her head and began to back out of the store. As she did, she backed into a small decorative table by the cash counter and a frame fell over. Thankfully it did not break.

"Oh! I'm sorry!" She picked up the photo hastily and then froze. "Who is this?"

The boy gave the picture a quick glance.

"Oh, that's my mom's mom. Actually, her name was Alexandra too." He smiled a faraway smile. "Before she died, she used to have all of us over for supper every single Sunday, even when it got to be over twenty-five cousins and grandkids. She would make quilts for all the kids. She taught everyone how to bake. And she was always in everyone's business. Nothing happened in our family without Grandma Alex knowing about it. She really was the glue who kept us all together." His eyes clouded over for a moment and he cleared his throat. Melissa nodded slowly and carefully put the frame back onto the small podium but not before she took one last glance at Alexandra and Andrew's wedding photo. Alexandra was instantly recognizable, wearing an ecstatic smile and the mystical dress that Melissa was carrying in a paper bag.

Elyse

Melissa did something she never did; she called in sick to work as soon as she walked out of the store. She was awash with a sea of emotions she could not comprehend and she felt like she needed to go home and be alone with her thoughts. Once she slipped over the threshold into the house, she carefully removed the dress from its packaging and stared at it. Again, it seemed to have a hypnotic affect on her. She placed it over the couch and sat down, idly stroking the cover of the book. She wondered how Alexandra had adopted such a different outlook after feeling so strongly about Andrew's family. She opened the diary to read the words she had already almost completely committed to memory. To her complete shock, the writing was no longer Alexandra's. In its place was an even, feminine scrawl which read Elyse, 1962. Confused, Melissa thumbed through the pages, individually, but Alexandra's words were gone as if they had never been there in the first place. She rubbed her eyes in disbelief and began to read.

April 14

Sam and I are getting hitched! Hee haw! It's about time! He proposed at the protest and everyone cheered. It was the most romantic thing in the world. I can't wait to spend the rest of my life with him! We have decided to elope. We're too broke to have a big wedding. His mom hates me anyway so I can't wait to see the look on her face when we tell her we got married behind her back. His brother is going to be a witness and my sister. We're doing it next month. Going upstate and finding a little church in the country. It is going to be the most beautiful ceremony. I can hardly wait!

April 20

We are looking at houses for sale. Sam said that we need at least four bedrooms for the children. He's such a joker. We aren't having kids. We don't need anyone else but us.

May 1

I think Sam genuinely wants to start a family. He keeps making little jokes about it but I sense a truth behind his words. I wonder if we're doing the right thing. I don't want to disappoint him but I don't want children. I thought he understood that.

May 10

We are leaving on Friday for upstate. Sam's brother took him out for his bachelor party and Sam's sister-in-law Mary came to stay with me and my sister. She brought her daughter and son along. They were such good, well-behaved children for ones so young. They were nothing like how my sister and I were at that age. Mary also brought me a gorgeous gift. It was the most spectacular wedding gown I have ever seen. It looks so expensive and Mary told me that there is a colorful history surrounding it. She warned me that it can only be worn if I promise to live my life with Sam according to God's plan and after I set eyes on it, I would have agreed to anything she made me promise. I can't think of a better way to become Mrs. Samuel Boswell.

Once again, the book came to an abrupt end. No further entries. Nothing to hint at what may have happened to Elyse. Well, I guess I'm going to have to find out for myself. Melissa pulled out the phone book and began looking for Boswell. To her surprise, there were a mere four listings but only one of them was S. Boswell. Before she could stop herself, Melissa was dialing the number at her fingers. Hang up! What are you doing? But before her hands could obey her brain, someone breathlessly answered the phone.

"Hello!"

"Uh...hi...is Elyse Boswell home?"

"Yep! Mom! Mom? It's for you!"

There was a click as someone picked up the extension.

"Hello?"

"Not you, idiot! It's for mom. MOM!" There was a click as the second person replaced the receiver. A moment later there was another click.

"Hello?" a young girl this time.

"Are you people deaf? IT'S FOR MOM! Are you mom? Hang up the phone, stupid face!" And then there was silence as both parties hung up in Melissa's ear. So she married him and had three children...at least? Melissa looked back at the dress. Was the garment God's way of ensuring the women who wore it lived happy, fulfilled lives? She turned back to the book. She hadn't even closed it yet like before with Alexandra, the careful script that Elyse had written was gone. And Melissa was staring at someone else's words.

Amber

This one was harder to read as the writing was nearly illegible. But Melissa pulled her lids into slits and surged through, anxious to read the next story.

Amber, 1997

March 11

The day is getting closer! I have no idea what I'm going to do for a dress! We went way over budget with the dj and bar. My mom says I can wear her dress but it is ugly! I didn't tell her that though. She's still mad I refuse to get married in a church. She doesn't understand that Eddy and I are atheists. I only have three weeks left to find something!

March 19th

Wow! I found the most amazing dress in a trunk in grandma's attic. She says she has no idea how it got there but she told me she doesn't like it for me. She begged me not to wear it for some reason. Old people are weird. I don't care. I need a dress and it's a perfect fit. A little old fashioned maybe but still beautiful. I'm getting married! Yay!

That was it. Two chicken scratched scribbles and absolutely nothing else...except...as Melissa sifted through the book, a small square of paper slipped out and onto her lap. All of the blood rushed out of her face when she realized what she was holding. It was Amber's obituary. Dead at thirty-two. She shouldn't have worn the dress, Melissa thought mournfully, taking in the woman's dark eyes and shiny hair. She had no intention of following God's plan and look what happened. Shaken to her core, Melissa stood up, trembling, trying to gather her thoughts. Dear Lord, what does this mean? Am I to marry Greg regardless of how many doubts I have? She suddenly was desperate to see Greg. She flung open the door and a clap of thunder made her jump. Steadying her nerves, she ran down the street to his house and pounded on the door. His mother answered and told her that he was still at the construction site. Running now, Melissa caught the bus as it turned the corner and headed toward downtown. Shivering, she huddled in the back of the near empty vessel. When the droplets on her face dried, she looked up and was staring into the gray eyes of the woman she had encountered earlier in the week. The woman opened her mouth to say something but was interrupted as someone shouted,

"Elyse? Elyse Boswell? Is that you? How the heck is Sam? How are the kids?" The woman looked at the man calling for attention and Melissa suddenly felt everything in her world connect.

She scurried the ten blocks from the bus stop to the job site where Greg was just packing up with the crew. He looked concerned as he saw her approaching.

"Melissa, are you – ?"

She flung herself into his arms and kissed him warmly.

"I'm fine. I just wanted to be near you." Greg looked touched by her words. He stared at her hopefully.

"Hey, guess what? They hired me on full time starting Monday!"

"That's amazing, sweetheart. I love you, Gregory Bond. I don't care where we get married or how we get married, as long as we are together.

There is nothing we can't overcome together." His face broke into a huge grin and he returned her embrace.

"I love you too, Melissa Bond."

For the first time in three days, the rain abruptly came to a complete stop and the sun parted the dismal clouds as if God himself was pre-blessing their nuptials.

Melissa

How strange to have found such a lovely gown in a dumpster and yet that is exactly where the homeless lady claimed she had discovered the satin and lace attire. The timing could not have been better. Lisette was running out of time to find a dress and the pressure of the wedding was affecting both she and Daniel. They were bickering constantly, often over the pettiest subjects and while they were both aware of this, they seemed unable to stop. Things were getting worse and Lisette found herself questioning their relationship more and more. The bag lady had made a prophetic statement before handing her the dress outside the 7-11.

"You can wear have this dress but you must always follow God's will in your marriage. Do you promise?" Lisette had nodded vehemently and promised. With the dress had come a beat up leather bound book as well. When she arrived home, Lisette quickly tried on the dress for size and was thrilled to find it fit perfectly as if it were made for her. Then she turned to the book and opened it up. It read Melissa, 2016.

LOVINA'S HEART

DEIDRA SCOTT

Chapter One

Lovina Miller took a deep breath as she reached up to pull a piece of laundry from the clothesline and put it in the basket at her feet. Above her head, a pair of bluebirds danced through the bright June sky, reminding her that summer was quickly approaching.

Summer. It was a time full of fresh starts and new beginnings.

Looking across the yard, Lovina watched David Yoder working with one of her brothers. Together, the two young men were struggling with their task, trying to break her *daed's* new horse.

Ach, just watching David sent a thrill of excitement through Lovina's heart. Although she had known him most of her life, there was something about him that could still put a spark inside of her, giving her the feeling that they had just met.

Growing up, Lovina had always dreamed of marrying David. It had just seemed natural to her. With their two houses located side-by-side, they had spent all of their childhood hours playing together in the creek that wound between their properties and climbing the big apple tree like little monkeys.

Lovina had decided early on that she and David would grow old together, spending their adult days raising babies and making a life within their Amish community.

Now that Lovina had turned eighteen-years-old, she felt like she was stuck in the midst of a waiting game, simply counting down the hours until David came forward to begin their relationship together.

Smiling to herself, Lovina basked in the realization that, as an adult, it was now time to watch her childhood dreams start to unfold.

"*Danki* for the help, David!" Lovina heard her father call out from the barn and looked up in time to see David waving goodbye to her family as he started across the yard.

Lovina felt her heart go aflutter when, rather than take the path back to his own parents' house, David veered closer to her own home and made a bee-line right for the clothesline where she was working.

"*Gut* afternoon, David!" Lovina called out, her voice seeming somewhat weak to her own ears.

Watching him come closer, Lovina couldn't help but marvel at how handsome her childhood friend had become. With a head-full of dark red hair and sparkling blue eyes, David had always looked like a cheerful storybook character; however, as he aged, he grew tall and muscular, his boyish looks transforming into that of a good-looking man.

"Hello there, Lovina," David called back, rolling down his sleeves as he walked along, "I tell you, that horse of your *daed's* nearly got me down this time!"

Lovina smiled as she pulled a pair of her brother's pants off of the laundry line and tossed them in the basket, "I guess we should consider ourselves glad to have such a good horse-breaker living so near-by."

To her surprise, David's face suddenly seemed to darken. Taking a deep breath, he reached up and put one hand on the clothesline, "Actually, Lovina, I wanted to talk to you about that."

Although Lovina had hoped that David would want to talk to her alone, she could already tell that his news wasn't going to be what she had wanted to hear.

"Lovina," David looked out across the fields, "Ever since you had your birthday, I'd been hoping..." his voice trailed off and he gave a shrug, "Well, nothing I'd hoped for is going to work out this summer." Standing up taller, he announced, "My uncle from Indiana wrote telling about the need for a good horse-trainer in his community. I agreed to go help for the next three months...I'll be home in time to help my dad get started on the harvest."

Lovina felt her heart drop in her chest. The idea that David would leave had never entered her mind. Even though it was only for three months, it felt like it might as well be three years.

"*Ach*, Lovina, don't be so sad," David reached out and placed his hand on her arm, "I'll be back – I promise. Kentucky is my home...I sure don't have any plans to run off for good."

Something about having his hand on her arm made the pain a little more bearable. Looking up, Lovina met David's tender gaze with her own.

"When I come back..." David took a deep breath and kicked at a clump of grass with his foot. It was strange to see him so uncomfortable – David was usually one to be bold and daring, willing to say whatever was necessary.

"When I come back, I hope we can spend more time together," David managed to say, "Seems like we've grown apart over the years, and I'm ready for that to end."

Lovina couldn't stop the smile that spread across her face, "And maybe not be climbing trees this time?" She added.

David laughed, "Of course we'll be climbing trees again!" He teased.

Growing more sober, he lifted his hand and ran it gently across her cheek, "I'll see you in three months, 'Vina."

Three months. As she watched him walk away and back to his parents' farm across the creek, Lovina took a deep breath and tried to still her thumping heart. Three months was a long time – she was just glad that she had those tender moments to cling to during the summer that stretched out before her.

Chapter Two

Taking a deep breath, David watched out the passenger window as the driver he had hired took him farther and farther from his home in Kentucky and on toward his Uncle Amos' house in Indiana.

"Are you nervous about leaving home for so long?" David's paid driver, Mr. Simpson asked, as he flipped his turn signal on and proceeded toward Uncle Amos' house.

David shook his head and laughed, "*Ach*, no, not nervous."

"Anxious to get away from your parents?" Mr. Simpson asked with a chuckle.

"No, nothing like that." David assured him, "Just glad to be helping my uncle and the people in his community."

Leaning his head back against the headrest of the seat, David closed his eyes and thought about Mr. Simpson's question.

Was he glad to be getting away from his parents? Although he had been quick to assure his driver that wasn't he case, David wasn't so certain himself. To be completely honest, David wasn't a bit sorry to be leaving for the summer. While he had always loved his home and his family, David relished the chance to get away.

Since David had been a little boy, he had always known what was expected of him. He was going to settle down, buy a piece of property close to his parents, and marry Lovina Miller. It wasn't a bad plan at all, but it seemed so boring and dull. Deep in his heart, David had always dreamed of excitement and adventure. Maybe his trip to Indiana would finally provide him with a chance to enjoy his freedom before he settled down for good.

David's driver took him straight to Uncle Amos' house, helped him unload his bags, and then left him to head back to Kentucky.

Uncle Amos and his entire family were happy to welcome David to their home. Uncle Amos explained that everyone in the community could use his horse breaking services and that they would be bringing their horses to his house so that David could train them. Uncle Amos also said that, during David's spare time he could help the family out in the dry goods store they had located in a small shed next to the road.

"I'll take you out to the store now, so that I can show you what kind of work you can do out there." Uncle Amos suggested once David had put his clothes away in the spare bedroom.

Leading David across the yard, Uncle Amos explained, "Of course, I will pay you for helping in the store...and you can also have all the money for training the horses."

David shook his head, "*Ach,* that's too much, Uncle Amos. I'm happy to have the chance to help out."

Uncle Amos chuckled and reached out to give David a slap on the back, "Now, now, don't go talking like that. I'm sure a handsome young man like you should be saving back to buy a nice farm and making plans for the future. I'd dare say that some pretty girl back home has caught your eye."

David gave a shrug, not too anxious to think about his future, "Nothing set in stone just yet."

The graveled lane ended and the two men found themselves standing side-by-side outside of the dry goods store. Reaching out, Uncle Amos pushed the door open, revealing a building with shelves full of baking supplies, canned goods, and some craft items.

"Hannah!" Uncle Amos called out, as he led David through the small building, "Hannah!"

"I'm over here," a soft voice returned.

Turning the corner around one of the shelves, they found a young Amish woman on her knees, busy stacking bags of flour.

"Hannah, I want you to meet my nephew, David," Uncle Amos announced, "David, this is Hannah – she is my wife's cousin and she's helping us out in the store this summer."

Hannah pulled herself to her feet and turned to stare up at David with large, blue eyes. Wisps of dark hair had escaped her prayer *kapp*, making a sort of halo around her face.

Just looking at her, David felt his heart give a leap. She was so unexpectedly beautiful in a dark, mysterious way.

"*Gut* to meet you, David," Hannah replied timidly.

"David is likely to be helping out in the store when he isn't working with the horses," Uncle Amos explained. Giving David a pat on the arm, he motioned toward the back room, "Come on, I want to show you where I store the bulk supplies."

As David followed his uncle, he had a hard time even listening to what was being said. His mind was still mesmerized by the beautiful and timid young lady he had just met. David could hardly wait to get to know and learn more about Hannah.

Lovina sat on the edge of her bed, looking out across the fields of farmland through her bedroom window. Knowing that David was no longer in the house next-door left a hollow emptiness in Lovina's heart. In her eighteen-years, she had never gone a summer without seeing David.

Lovina tired to imagine what her sweet friend was doing at that moment. Did he realize how much she was thinking of him? Did he miss her at all?

Lovina closed her eyes and took a deep breath, "Dear God," she whispered into the darkness, "Please, bring the man that I love back to me."

Chapter Three

David carefully guided his uncle's buggy down the road. It was only his second day in Indiana and work was already starting to pick up; however, Uncle Amos had sent him to town to pick up some nails for a woodworking project he was doing in the barn.

The summer afternoon sun shone down on David and the warmth of the breeze put a smile on his face. David was enjoying his time away from home and, although he had not had many opportunities to spend time with Hannah, he had hopes that would change eventually.

The buggy suddenly took a lung, pulling David out of his thoughts.

"Woah, boy! Woah!" David pulled tightly on the reigns, unsure of what was happening to the buggy. Carefully guiding the horse to the side of the road, he jumped down from his seat and looked over the situation.

Something was wrong with the front buggy wheel. Grabbing a hold of it, David gave it a wiggle, trying to determine if it could keep going.

Pulling off his straw hat, David slapped it against his leg in frustration. He couldn't get to town on that wheel and he didn't think he could make it back to his uncle's house either.

The clipping of oncoming horse hooves made David stand up straighter and wave desperately at the approaching buggy.

The driver was a single Amish man. As soon as David caught his attention, the other driver pulled his buggy to the side of the road behind David.

"Hi there!" David greeted with a smile as he watched the other Amish man get off his buggy and start toward him, "Boy, I sure am glad to see you!" Sticking out a hand, he announced, "I'm David Yoder. I'm staying with my Uncle Amos Yoder – you probably know him."

The stranger nodded and simply said, "I'm Luke Christner." Taking a deep breath, he walked over to the buggy and squatted down to inspect the wheel.

"Looks like this is busted good," he announced, pushing his hat back on his head and reaching up to wipe some sweat from his brow.

David groaned, "I was afraid of that."

Standing to his feet, Luke continued, "I'm afraid you shouldn't drive it any farther than just a few feet or you'll end up wrecking or destroying your entire buggy." With a slight smirk, Luke added, "Lucky for you, this is my parents' drive right up ahead. And I just happen to work on buggies for a living."

David's eyes got large and he let out a huge sigh, "Oh, *gut*! Do you think that you could help me out?"

Luke nodded, "Sure thing. Just lead your buggy down to my workshop. I'll have her fixed up in just a bit."

True to his word, Luke had the buggy wheel fixed within an hour.

David stayed by the young man who had rescued him and worked to fill him in on all the details about his life, his home, and his family. Luke, who seemed to be more reserved, was happy to listen and donate very few details of his own.

"How much do I owe you?" David asked as Luke put the repaired wheel back on his buggy.

Luke gave a shrug as he secured the wheel in place, "Nothing. Consider it a welcome present. Maybe you can help me with one of my horses one day this summer."

"*Ach*," David raised an eyebrow, "I can't let you do that. I took some time you could have been working on other projects..."

Before he could finished, Luke started shaking his head, "No, no you didn't," he assured David as he stood up straight, "Honestly, I didn't have any other work for today." Sighing deeply, he announced, "As badly as we need a horse trainer in this area, we do not need any kind of buggy work. Jobs around here are scarce, David. I was glad to help."

David pondered Luke's statement for a moment. As an idea entered his mind, a broad smile spread across his face, "Listen, Luke! You may not be needed here, but you sure would be in my community! How would you feel about going to Kentucky to spend the summer with my family? It would sure help them out while I'm gone, and you could earn money doing buggy repairs and carpentry work!"

Luke was silent, obviously studying David's suggestion. Finally, with a shrug, he announced, "*Jah* – I don't see why that wouldn't be great. *Danki*, David."

The entire plan made David's face light up like that of a little boy. Grinning from ear-to-ear, he grabbed his new friend's hand in a shake and started making plans to get Luke back to Kentucky.

Chapter Four

Lovina reached up to wipe some sweat from her forehead as she took a break from chopping weeds out of the row of green beans. Despite all her hard work, the weeds were quickly starting to overtake the plants.

David had now been gone two weeks, and Lovina had yet to hear anything from him. His absence made her sad and she wished for all she was worth that she would receive a letter.

Glancing across the field toward his house, she thought of all the times they had snuck away from their chores and played together instead.

To her surprise, Lovina saw a young man approaching her. Could it be…? Lovina's heart dropped as he drew closer. Although she had hoped that it was David, she instantly realized that her eyes had been playing tricks on her. This stranger was even taller than her dear childhood friend and slightly thinner.

"Hullo," Lovina called out as he continued to draw closer.

"Hullo," the stranger returned, his voice deep and almost mysterious, "Are you Lovina Miller?"

Lovina stood up straighter and adjusted her prayer *kapp*, "That would be me. Do I know you?"

The stranger shook his head, "No, you don't." Now he was so close that Lovina was able to get a good look at him. This strange Amish man looked to be in his early twenties, but he seemed more mature. His brown hair was so dark it was almost black, and his eyes a dark color chocolate. Just looking at him made Lovina take a deep breath of surprise. *Ach*, it was hard to remember a time that she had ever seen such a *gut*-looking man!

"I'm Luke Christner. I know your friend, David, and I'm staying with his family until he returns." Glancing toward her house, Luke asked, "Is your *daed* at home? The Yoders told me that he has a construction crew and I'd like a job."

Lovina felt so out of sorts, she wasn't sure what to do. Looking down at her bare feet, she tried to gather her composure. Taking a deep breath, she said, "*Nee*, my *daed* isn't home from work yet, but we're expecting him any minute. If you'd like to wait in the house, my *mamm* can give you some fresh lemonade and cookies."

Luke glanced from the house back to Lovina and then shrugged, "If you don't mind, I'll just stay out here. Looks like you could use some help." Grabbing for an extra hoe, Luke set to work, removing the pesky weeds from among the rows of bean plants.

There was something about Luke that made Lovina feel uncertain about everything. He was a good help in the garden, but she certainly would have felt more at-ease without him. On the other hand, she dreaded him leaving once her father got home from work. Just being near him made her feel things that she had never experienced – she found herself overwhelmed by a sort of giddiness that sprung up from deep within. Although Lovina had always been a talker, she suddenly seemed almost speechless.

"You don't have to do this," Lovina assured him.

Luke simply set his jaw and turned to look at her with his brooding, dark eyes, "I don't have to...but I want to."

Lovina felt weak in the knees, as if she might keel right over. Taking a deep breath, she tried to stead herself.

Suddenly, she found herself a little glad that David was going to be gone for the summer. As quickly as the thought flitted through her mind, she pushed it away; however, just the realization that she could think such a thing left Lovina questioning everything about the future.

David washed his hands in a pail of water that had been set out by the barn, preparing himself for the evening meal. Inside the house, Aunt Miriam was putting the finishing touches on a pot of homemade chili with the help of three of David's cousins.

True to Uncle Amos' word, in the time that David had spent in Indiana he had already been so busy, he hardly had time to even think about being at home.

Wiping his clean hands on a towel, David glanced across the acres of land that his uncle owned. There, in the glowing darkness of the evening, he could make out the form of a young woman walking near the pond.

Hannah.

David had learned to recognize her from a distance. Even though it would be hard to distinguish her from any other Amish woman from so far away, David could pick Hannah out because she was always alone. It seemed like she carried an air of sadness with her, wherever she went.

Taking a deep breath, David stepped out of the barn and started the short walk to the pond.

"Hi there," David called out as he drew near to Hannah.

The young woman looked up at him and gave a sad smile.

"What are you doing?"

Hannah gave a shrug and pulled her black shawl tighter against her shoulders, "I just felt like a walk," she explained.

David stepped up next to her side, "It must be sort of lonely to walk all alone."

Hannah shrugged again, "I'm used to being alone."

David *thought* over his childhood and how little time he had ever spent just to himself. There were always siblings to play with, other Amish children to enjoy at events, and Lovina. Lovina had always been there for him.

Just the thought of his old friend's name sent a nagging sense of guilt through his mind.

Hadn't he promised Lovina that, when he got home, things would be different? Hadn't he promised that they would spend time together? So, what was he doing, trying to get closer to Hannah?

"David..." Hannah's soft voice brought him out of his thoughts, "Are you all right, David? I've never seen you so solemn and quiet."

David looked up at her in surprise, his face breaking out in a broad grin, "Oh, *jah*, I'm fine. I was just thinking is all."

"I didn't know you were able to do that...you know, think without saying what was going through your mind." Although Hannah's words were haughty, David *looked* up in time to catch a teasing smile cross her lips. It was the first time he had ever seen her smile and, something about it made him want to see it a thousand times more.

"Maybe it's too much time around you," David suggested, "Because I don't think you ever say anything much at all."

Hannah's tender smirk turned into a broad smile and David was, once again, captivated by her charm.

Reaching out, he gently took her elbow in his hand, "Would you do me the honor of letting me walk with ya tonight?"

Hannah was silent for a moment, studying David for all that he was worth. Finally, she nodded slowly and said, "*Jah* – I suppose that might be nice."

Chapter Five

Just as David had predicted, it was easy for Luke to find work in Kentucky. He not only spent his afternoons working on buggies in the Yoder's empty shed, but also joined the carpentry work crew lead by Lovina's father.

Lovina wasn't exactly sure how it happened, but it seemed that she and Luke were constantly thrown in the paths of one another. Lovina tried to convince herself that it was merely a coincidence, but she had to admit that it was more than that.

The longer David was gone, the less she was thinking about him and the more she was thinking about Luke.

When he wasn't busy with work, Luke frequently dropped by to help Lovina in the garden; although he wasn't a talker, there was something about his calm attitude that left Lovina yearning for more time with him.

One evening, Lovina baked a plate of her famous homemade ginger snap cookies and decided to take a few across the creek as a thank you for Luke's help in the garden.

Knocking on the shed door, she cautiously pushed it open, cheerfully announcing, "Hello! Luke! Are ya in here?"

"*Jah*, I'm here," Luke replied.

There he was, standing next to a work bench with a busted buggy wheel laid out in front of him.

"Hi there!" Lovina greeted him, suddenly feeling unsure of herself and terribly bashful, "I thought I might bring you something." Placing the plate of cookies on the work table, she watched Luke eyeball them before picking one up and putting it in his mouth.

"It's just a thank you for all the help you've been giving me," she explained.

Luke raised his eyebrows and nodded as he swallowed, "*Danki* – they're very good. You're a good baker, Lovina."

Lovina felt her heart skip a beat with his compliment. Looking at the work he was doing, she added, "Looks like you've got quite a few talents of your own."

Reaching for another cookie, Luke gave a shrug, "I keep busy for sure....but that's a good thing. I'm always thankful for the money."

Leaning back against the table, Lovina studied him in the growing darkness, "Saving back for a farm of your own?"

Luke stared straight at his work and shook his head, "No. I'm going to give my money to help out my family. I have no need of a place of my own."

"Don't you ever hope to get married and have a family?"

Luke shook his head slowly, "I'm afraid all of my dreams are gone. I plan to be alone forever."

His words broke Lovina's heart. Although he tried to sound resolved, it was easy to hear the pain in his voice.

"*Ach*, Luke," she managed to whisper with a smile, "Don't say that. You never know what might happen."

Luke took in a deep breath and then let it out slowly. Looking up to meet Lovina's eyes, he studied her for what seemed minutes before asking, "What about you? Do you think that you could ever love someone like me?"

His question took Lovina by such surprise that she almost fell over. Her eyes growing large, she looked down at the floor, her heart flooded by a million different emotions.

"I...I...Luke..." Lovina's voice was trailing in every direction but her words were making no sense at all.

"Lovina," Reaching out, Luke put his hand on top of hers, "Would you consider going with me to the singing after church this weekend?"

It felt like Lovina would not be able to breath, so many decisions were running helter-skelter through her mind. Almost a surprise to herself, she heard her voice say, "Sure. I don't see why not."

Although David had been staying busy with the horses, he still managed to make some time to help out in the store. With a beautiful girl like Hannah there, he had to find time to spend with her.

One afternoon they had received a large order of supplies and were hurrying to put them on the shelves before it would be too dark to see, even by the glow of the lantern.

"*Ach*, this is a job!" David grumbled as he hurried to put some bags of flour in their place on a shelf, "Of course this would just happen to be the night that Uncle Amos and his entire family went visiting...leaving you and me to do all the work."

Hannah smiled and shook her head, "David, you complain so much. I don't mind the work. Work keeps me busy...work keeps my mind off of...other things."

Suddenly interested, David looked up in surprise. Maybe he would finally have a chance to hear some of the secrets that were hidden away behind this mysterious girl's sad blue eyes.

"What other things?" David asked.

Hannah shrugged as she ran her fingers over a bag of sugar, "Disappointments...heartbreaks...bad decisions."

Hannah went silent, assuring David that he would hear no more of her story, but then she surprised him when she went on to clear her throat and say, "I had a boyfriend...a fiancé even."

As the words came pouring out of her mouth, it was easy to see that they were tearing her apart. Hannah closed her eyes and continued, "But things didn't work out. We were engaged but...well, I was filled with so many uncertainties. I called off the wedding before it was even announced in church. I didn't mean to end everything with him – I just needed more time to think. But I'm afraid he took it as an outright rejection. And now, I'll never have a chance with him again," Hannah reached up to wipe away the tears that were threatening to overwhelm her, "*Ach*, David, it almost breaks my heart to talk about it. I have destroyed all my chances for happiness."

Looking at her in the light of the lantern, her face clouded over with pain and tears gathering in her eyes, David felt totally broken for her. Pulling himself to his feet, he stood up straight and stepped closer to her, putting a hand on her thin shoulder.

"Hannah," he whispered her name with all the tenderness that he had been storing in his heart, "Dear Hannah...you still have a thousand chances for happiness." Reaching up, he took his thumb and brushed a tear off of her cheek.

Hannah took a deep breath and let it out slowly. Looking at him in surprise, she simply whispered, "*Danki*, David." Then she squared her shoulders and announced, "Let's get back to work."

Chapter Six

Over the next few days, David and Hannah had little time to spend together. He looked forward to ever chance he had to see her. Although their friendship had not had time to progress, David felt confident that over the rest of the summer he could easily earn himself a special place in Hannah's lonely heart.

One afternoon, David had finally found a chance to work in the dry goods store alongside Hannah when one of his cousins came rushing into the shed with a letter in his outstretched hand.

"David," the little cousin called out, "You got some mail!"

Taking the letter, David quickly recognized the handwriting as that of his younger sister, Lydia.

Ripping the seal open, David pulled out the letter, unsure why his teenage sister would even take the time to write him.

Dear David,

I don't want to bother you while you're gone, but I need to let you know something important. I've always thought that you and Lovina had something special together, although I'm not sure if you had any kind of plans for the future or an agreement. While you've been gone, Lovina has taken a spark to the very man you sent here to work – Luke Christner. Seems like they're seeing each other almost every day and last night I overheard him invite her to the singing Sunday night. She agreed to go with him.

I don't mean to stick my nose in where it doesn't belong, but I know that you were always sweet on Lovina and just thought you should know.

Your sister,

Lydia

"*Ach,*" David read over the letter and then reread it again, his heart suddenly dropping into his stomach.

Lovina – with Luke? A multitude of emotions suddenly assailed David. He found himself so frustrated, almost angry at Luke for stealing his girl. How dare Luke go to David's own home and try to take the woman he loved away from him? David was hurt, so hurt, by Lovina's decision to move forward with a relationship with someone else. But, worst of all, David felt incredible guilt and sadness.

Deep in his heart, David realized that it was his own fault that Lovina and Luke were growing close. In all the time that David had been in Indiana, he had never taken the time to even write his childhood sweetheart a letter – he had just always taken for granted that she would be there for him when he returned.

While he had been busy pursing a friendship with Hannah, he had never thought that Lovina might be looking at someone else.

Reaching up, David rubbed his hand across his face, trying to gather his wits and decide what to do next.

"What is wrong, David?" Hannah asked softly as she stepped up next to him.

David balled his free hand up into a fist, fighting the urge to destroy the letter he had just received. Passing it to Hannah, he quickly explained, "I don't know how to tell you this, Hannah, but Lovina...well, she and I have always been friends. I don't mean to have led you astray in any way because I have liked you since the day we met but this..." David couldn't go on.

Hannah took the letter in her own hands and read it slowly, her eyes growing large as she went over the message again and again.

"David," she managed to breath softly, "What are you going to do?"

David brushed his hand through his hair as memories of Lovina ran across his mind, "I don't know. I just don't know." Turning, he gave the floor a hard kick with the toe of his boot.

"David," Hannah took a deep breath and shook her head slowly, "I hate to say this, but you know that we aren't meant to be together. No matter how happy we might have both been to pretend...it just isn't so. You have made my summer much more enjoyable...but it's time to get back to our real lives."

David looked down at his feet. He wanted to fight her words; he hated the idea of giving Hannah up completely. But, when he thought of his dear Lovina...he knew that he couldn't live without her.

"Go to her, David!" Hannah exclaimed, "Go to Lovina and let her know that you love her."

Taking a deep breath, David nodded his head, "I'll go call a driver right now."

Chapter Seven

David sat in the passenger seat of the truck, half-heartedly listening as his driver talked incessantly during the long trip back home. Looking out the window, David watched the scenery slowly change from the flat Amish country of Indiana to the rolling hills of Kentucky.

With each mile that passed, it seemed that David got even more nervous about his future with Lovina.

When he first started home, he had been certain that she would be glad to see him but now…well, the closer he got to her, the less sure he became. Maybe she had truly fallen for Luke and she wouldn't want to even see him. Maybe David had blown his one and only chance for true love with the only girl he ever truly cared for.

Lovina had just filled up a bucket of water and got down on her knees to scrub the kitchen floor with a scrub brush when she heard a truck pull up in the front yard.

Ach, Lovina thought to herself as she plunged her hands down into the soapy water, *Daed must have visitors.*

It was Saturday afternoon and Lovina found her mind plagued with thoughts of Luke and their upcoming date. Although she truly enjoyed spending time with him, there was something about agreeing to go on a date with him that put her mind entirely in a tizzy. As much as she liked Luke and was attracted to him, Lovina battled thoughts of David – it seemed so sad to be turning her back on their relationship with each other.

But, she reasoned to herself, when she thought back on it, she and David had never had a true relationship. Sure, he had always been a good friend to her, but it seemed that was all things were to ever be. Since he left for Indiana, she had not heard a word from him and, as sad as she was to admit it, she was starting to wonder if he would ever come home at all.

"Lovina."

The voice seemed to come out of no where. Lovina looked up in surprise, wondering if she was truly hearing a person or if it was her own imagination.

There, standing in the doorway to the kitchen, was David himself.

"David!" Lovina managed to breathe as she struggled to pull herself to her feet, "Oh, David…is that really you?"

In an instant, David had bridged the space between them. He came right to her side, nearly knocking her bucket of soapy water over in his hurry.

"Lovina," David managed to say, somewhat louder this time, "Lovina…" he seemed to want to say more, but acted as if he couldn't find the words. Reaching out, he grabbed Lovina and gathered her into his arms.

To Lovina, everything felt like a crazy dream. Pressed firmly against her old friend's body, all thoughts of Luke vanished from her mind as she let David hold her like a little girl.

"Lovina," David pulled back only long enough to kiss her on the mouth, "Lovina, I have been a total moron. I am so sorry!"

"David," Lovina managed to say as she tried to catch her breath, "David…what has happened?"

David stepped back as he struggled to gather his composure. Reaching up, he wiped away at tears that threatened to overtake him.

"Lovina," he reached out and held her hands in his own, "I have been so ignorant. I left home, anxious to find adventure and experience new things…and I almost lost the one thing that means the most to me in the world – you."

Lovina felt her heart start to melt as David poured out his soul to her, "Lovina, I love you. I love you more than I ever realized. I thought that Uncle Amos was giving me a chance to experience adventure but I think it was actually the good Lord allowing me the opportunity to realize how much I love you. Please, Lovina…I don't want to wait any longer. Say that you will marry me!"

There had never been anything that Lovina wanted more. In that instant, it felt like all of her hopes and dreams were finally coming true.

Luke.

The name entered her mind suddenly and it felt like the life was drained right out of her. Oh, but hadn't she already led him to believe that she cared for him? Hadn't she already agreed to go out on a date with him this very weekend?

"David," Lovina squeezed her dear friend's hands tightly as she looked for the right words to share her news, "David. I have been a foolish girl."

"And I have been a foolish man," David was quick to add.

Lovina smiled and shook her head, "Perhaps we've both been foolish..."

Her words were cut short as the sound of an approaching vehicle brought them both from their thoughts.

Glancing out the window, they watched together as a strange car stopped in front of the house and let out a passenger.

David felt his heart sink when he saw the visitor who was getting out of the strange car.

It was Hannah.

David thought that she had understood. What was she doing...following him all the way to Kentucky of all places? Hadn't she been the one who had said that their relationship wasn't going to work and even pushed him to return to Lovina? What was she doing here now?

David battled the urge to run forward and stop her before she could get to the house. Turning to Lovina, he struggled to find the words to explain what was surely about to come.

"Lovina..." he hurried to say, "While I was gone, I was an idiot. I hate telling you this more than you will ever know, but I got involved with a girl from Indiana. We never started to court, but we were heading in that direction when I heard that you and Luke had begun a relationship...."

As the words poured from his mouth, David watched Lovina's face turn ashen and then red with shame.

"You already know about Luke?" She managed to whisper.

David nodded his head, "That was the wake-up call I needed. That was what I needed to bring me back home. I never want to risk losing you again, Lovina!"

Lovina started to wipe tears away from her eyes, "David, I don't want to lose you either! But what you heard is true. Luke and I have grown close and are on the verge of starting a relationship. I was so foolish, David, but I was afraid I had lost you and now I don't know what to do..."

In the other room, they could hear a knock on the front door.

Wiping at her eyes, Lovina hurried to go open it with David trailing close behind. When she opened the door, Hannah was standing on the front porch, a determined look in her blue eyes.

"I need to talk to David," she announced, looking from Lovina to David.

"David," she took a deep breath, "I need to go to your house...I need to see Luke."

Luke? David was more confused than ever. Cocking his head to one side, he tried to understand where this strange twist came into play.

"You don't have to look far," the deep voice of Luke spoke out and they all turned in surprise to find that he had come up on the porch and was standing just out of view.

"Hannah," as he said the name, his voice seemed to fill with a strange sort of pain.

"*Ach*, Luke..." Hannah looked down at her black shoes as if she couldn't hold his gaze, "I have been wanting to talk to you."

Luke shook his head sadly, "I can't imagine what we would have to say to each other now."

"Luke...you know that I am a very shy girl," Hannah said in a shaky voice, "And I have let my fear get the better of me far too many times. I almost let it destroy what we had together. But Luke...I can't let that happen."

David's eyes got large as he realized that Luke must be the ex-beau that Hannah had told him about.

"I love you, Luke," Hannah announced resolutely, "I love you and I still want to be your wife...if you can ever find it in your heart to have me."

David watched Luke and held his breath, hoping that he would agree.

Stepping forward, Luke reached out and took Hannah in his arms, "I love you too, Hannah!" He exclaimed as he cupped her face in his hands, "I have always loved you and I always will." Turning to look at Lovina, he quickly tried to explain, "Lovina, I hope that you understand..."

Lovina smiled broadly as she wrapped her arms around David's waist, "It is fine, Luke. I think that things are exactly the way that they are supposed to be!"

Epilogue

Standing together at the kitchen sink, Lovina and David watched as a group of children played outside in their front yard.

"Look at those crazy things," Lovina muttered as she noticed her daughter trying to climb a tree.

"Just like us when we were little," David announced.

Lovina looked up at him and smirked, "*Jah* – and I think our little girl might have a crush on the neighbor boy, as well."

David and Lovina had now been married for ten years and had three children of their own. It had been a double wedding shared with Hannah and Luke, who decided to move to Kentucky so that Luke would continue to enjoy a steady stream of work.

David and Lovina had built their house behind his parents' place and, to their surprise, Hannah and Luke had bought a piece of farm land right across the creek.

Their children played together and it wouldn't be any surprise if someday those same children would grow up to marry one another.

David smiled broadly and gathered his wife up in his arms.

"I'm glad I went to Indiana that summer," he announced as he reached out to push a strand of her brown hair back from her face, "Because that summer showed me how much I need you in my life."

Bending over, he gave her a gentle kiss.

Life truly was as David and Lovina had always imagined it – and they were happier than they ever could have guessed possible.

THE END

The Prideful Amish Girl

Samantha Collier

The notes filled the barn, carrying a tide of joyful singing to the top of the roof.

It was a cold winter's day, and the small Amish community gathered to honour the Lord that Sunday were shivering with the cold.

Linda scratched her neck, trying to turn her collar up against the cold. She looked around her. Mr and Mrs Albrecht's breath was fogging with condensation as they sang. Their two young children were fidgeting with the cold. Mrs Albrecht leaned down to keep them still.

If only someone would close the door, Linda thought. The cold wind was swirling through the barn, and she was afraid that her grandfather might pass out. He was wrapping his coat around himself, swaying slightly. He had suffered a stroke recently, and Linda found herself constantly checking on him ever since.

As if in answer to her silent plea, someone slipped away from the congregation and closed the door. She turned her head slightly. It was Vernon Eicher. She smiled at him, in thank you. He seemed surprised, but smiled tentatively back.

It did the trick. The barn started to warm up, slightly.

Linda closed her eyes, thanking the Lord that the frigid breeze was gone .

The next hymn started. Oh, how she loved this one! She let her voice ring out pure and true, joy enveloping her as she sang. She could feel the eyes of people turning to her, but she didn't care.

When Linda was singing, it was as if the whole world was suspended.

She knew that she had a lovely voice; she had been told often enough. And it wasn't just church service or Evening Sing when she sang. As she did her chores at home, or walked in the woods, she would sing out loud just for the joy of it.

She would practise in her bedroom, standing in front of the mirror. Her mother would tell her off for that, telling her she was being vain. But Linda just thought of it as practise.

It was a communion with God, she knew. God wouldn't have given her such a lovely voice if he hadn't intended her to use it, now would he?

The hymn ended, and so did the service. People started talking, milling around to socialise before lunch.

Linda's best friend, Barbara, made her way to where Linda stood with her family.

"Linda!" she breathed. "You sang so beautifully in that last hymn. The hairs on the back of my neck were standing up. You have the voice of an angel!"

Linda smiled, enjoying the praise. "Thank you, Barbara," she replied. The two young women giggled together.

Afterwards, when everyone sat at the long outdoor tables to enjoy lunch, Linda called Barbara over to sit beside her.

"What do you think of Vernon Eicher?" she whispered to her friend, looking down the table at the young man sitting next to his father. Barbara followed her gaze.

"He is a very solemn young man," Barbara whispered back. "But very handsome! Linda, have you taken a shine to him?"

"Maybe," Linda replied. She stared at Vernon, who felt her gaze and turned her way. She smiled, and she was happy to see that Vernon returned her smile again.

"Linda Heiser."

She turned to see Mrs Albrecht addressing her. The woman was leaning over the table to catch Linda's attention.

"*Ja*, Mrs Albrecht?"

The woman smiled. "I just wanted to say, Linda, how much I admire your singing. You have the most beautiful voice."

Linda preened. She could feel everyone's eyes at the table on her again. She really did love the attention!

"Thank you, Mrs Albrecht," she replied, loudly. "I have practised a lot. But, yes, some people are just born with lovely voices. I think I am one of them."

She heard her mother, who was sitting on the other side of her, gasp.

"My teacher used to say I had the voice of a nightingale," Linda continued. "Old Miss Miller said I could rival the greatest singers of all time!" She puffed out her chest a bit as she spoke.

Her mother nudged her, underneath the table, but Linda ignored her.

"*Ja*, well." Mrs Albrecht's face had frozen slightly. She looked down at her plate.

Linda couldn't resist looking down the table to see if Vernon was listening.

He was. But his face had coloured slightly, and he avoided her eye.

Then she saw the face of his father, old Mr Eicher, staring at her. He was frowning, shaking his head slightly as he did so.

Linda momentarily felt shamed, then she tossed her head back. Who was anybody to comment on what she said about herself?

She had high self-esteem. She always had. She didn't see the point in putting herself down. And when it came to her voice, Linda was proud. She had been told often enough in her life how lovely it was. Why shouldn't she think so, too?

But she had a stab of misgiving when Vernon refused to catch her eye.

***

That night, after she had returned home after the Evening Sing, Linda made her way to her bedroom.

"I want to talk to you, young lady."

She turned around. Her mother, of course. Linda groaned inwardly. Here we go, she thought to herself. Another lecture.

"Linda, why must you persist in being so proud?" Her mother had her hands on her hips and her lips pursed.

Linda kept walking into her room, turning the kerosene lamp on.

She glanced at her mother, sighing. "Do we really have to do this, Mamm? I am tired! It's been a long day." As if to prove her point, she collapsed across the bed, flailing dramatically.

Mrs Heiser frowned. "*Ja*, we really have to do this, daughter of mine." She sat down on the side of the bed. "Linda, we have talked about this a lot. What you did today, at lunch, wasn't acceptable."

Linda looked at her mother. "What did I do?"

Mrs Heiser sighed. "Boasting. You know it was boasting."

Linda sat up, suddenly. "I don't see that it was," she said, crossly. "Mrs Albrecht gave me a compliment. It would have been rude to ignore it."

"There is a difference between taking a compliment," her mother continued, "and turning it into a boast. Saying that your teacher said you had a voice as good as the greatest singers is boasting."

"It's not!" Linda's eyes flashed. "She said it to me! I didn't lie!"

Mrs Heiser stood up. "I will not argue with you," she said. "I want you to pray tonight, and think of what I have said. Our Lord will show you the right way, if you let him." She walked out of the room, closing the door behind her.

Linda sighed again. Why was it always this way?

She knew that her community didn't like people to be prideful. She had been taught that since she was a very young girl.

But it was different when you had a gift, surely? A gift from God? God wanted his children to nurture their talents. That was why he gave them out.

She undressed slowly, praying before she retired.

"Dear Lord," she said, aloud. "Everyone says I am prideful. But why did you gift me with my voice if you didn't want me to be proud of it?

I don't understand." She didn't meditate any further on it. She climbed into bed and turned out the light.

She wouldn't think any more about it. Besides, other things were playing on her mind.

Vernon Eicher. Tonight, he had finally asked her out.

She thought of his dark hair and flashing dark eyes. He was so handsome! The handsomest man in her district. He had courted other girls, never glancing Linda's way. Finally, he had noticed her back. It was a dream come true.

She replayed their conversations over in her head until she finally fell asleep.

***

Vernon arrived shortly after six that Saturday night, ready to take Linda on their date.

Linda was buzzing with excitement, singing as she awaited him.

"Linda! Could you keep it down!" Her brother, Jacob, stuck his head out of the living room door, chiding her.

"Oh, Jacob, why do you always want to spoil my fun?" She twirled around him, laughing.

"Linda! A buggy is here!" Her mother grabbed her, smoothing down her dress as she did so.

Vernon came in, looking especially handsome in his dark suit.

"Where are you young people going tonight?" Her mother looked from one to the other expectantly.

"I am taking Linda to town, Mrs Heiser," Vernon replied. "I thought she might like to look at the Nativity scene in the centre after we have had dinner."

"Lovely," Mrs Heiser replied. "I hope you have a good evening."

"We will, darling Mamm," Linda laughed, kissing her mother on the cheek.

They had a wonderful time in town. Vernon took her to Mast's Diner, where they ate chicken pot pie and butter noodles, followed by a big helping of peach pie. Linda was relieved that conversation was easy, and they had a similar sense of humour, laughing at each other's jokes.

Afterwards, they walked to the town centre, where a beautiful Nativity scene had been set up, complete with life size sheep and the three Wise Kings.

"I always loved looking at Mary, the most," Linda whispered as they stood there. Twinkling lights framed the stable, resembling stars in the night sky.

"She seemed so calm and lovely, in her blue gown and veil, staring down at our Lord." Linda sighed. "Maybe because I always envied calm people. I have always had so much energy, racing from one thing to the next. My mind never stays still." She smiled, a little ruefully.

Vernon looked at her. "That is what I like about you," he said, slowly. "You are always smiling and full of life."

Linda smiled. "That is a lovely thing to say, Vernon," she whispered.

They stared at the Nativity a while longer, soaking in the tranquillity.

That night in bed, Linda could still see the lights twinkling in her head, like lanterns lighting the way to her future.

***

Linda was still dreaming of Vernon over her schapple at the breakfast table the next day.

"Linda!" Her mother nudged her. "Enough day dreaming! You have chores."

Linda nodded. Had she been so obvious?

Did he like her as much as she liked him? She replayed every word and gesture in her head. Yes, she thought. He does like me. But he hadn't suggested another date, an omission which troubled her.

"We have to go into town later, so make sure you have everything finished." Her mother got up, picking up the breakfast dishes as she did.

Linda brightened. They were going into town. That meant that she would be able to make an excuse and slip away to see Vernon. He worked in town, at Eicher's Furniture shop.

Later that day, after they had done their business, Linda turned to her mother.

"I might just go to the bakery," she said. "I could get us some of those cream pies that you like so much and meet you back at the buggy in half an hour?"

She turned and walked away before her mother could say yes or no.

The bakery was on the way to the furniture shop, so she would have enough time to get the cakes and still see Vernon – if he was there, of course.

It was another cold day. Linda turned the collar up on her coat, and put on her mittens. It would be a brisk walk.

The bell tinkled over the door of Eicher's as she entered.

He was here; she could see him in the back, turning the lathe on a table leg. Vernon was a talented furniture maker – her father often said he made the best wooden furniture in the district.

"*Ja*?" The assistant approached her, expectantly.

"Would I be able to go and say hello to Vernon?" She smiled brightly at the woman.

The woman was assessing her, somewhat coldly. "*Ja*, I suppose," she said, slowly. "But please be mindful that he is busy."

Linda walked away, into the back of the shop.

Vernon hadn't seen her, yet. What would he think, of her coming to see him like this? Would he think her too forward?

He looked up at that moment, and saw her. He stopped the lathe slowly.

Her smile wavered slightly. Was he pleased?

He got up, walking toward her. "Linda," he said. "Are you here to buy some furniture?"

She laughed. "Oh, Vernon, you know I can't tell a stool from a chair," she said. "I have just come to say hello." She looked down, feeling a bit awkward. "So, hello."

"Hello," he responded. But he wasn't smiling.

Oh dear. Had she misinterpreted his interest entirely?

"I just wanted to say thank you for a lovely evening," she blurted. "I had a lovely time."

He smiled, then. "I did too," he said. He was gazing at her, as if there was something else he wanted to say.

"Well, I suppose I should go." She looked around her. "You are busy." Ask me out on another date, she thought to herself. Could she will him to do it?

"Would you like to go sledding after work tomorrow?" He looked at her. "There is enough snow on the fields now, I think."

She smiled. "Oh yes!" She looked up at him. "Will you pick me up?"

"*Ja*, be ready around four," he said.

"See you then," she said, walking out of the shop. He did like her! She was grinning widely now. She knew it!

Vernon watched her walk out of the shop. He was deep in thought, and hadn't heard his father approaching.

"Was that the Heiser girl?" Mr Eicher, his father, was standing there, staring disapprovingly at the door.

"It was," Vernon answered, glancing at his father. What would he say?

"You know how I feel about her," Mr Eicher continued. "That girl is too prideful. She doesn't act with the modesty that a young girl should. Always boasting about her singing. You shouldn't court her, Vernon. What about Emma Sommer? She is a modest girl, always respectful."

"I don't really like Emma," Vernon said. He looked at his father. "But I do like Linda. I know what you mean about her boasting – she can be prideful. But could I talk to her about it, see if I can get her to see how pride is wrong?"

Mr Eicher frowned. "I don't know, Vernon. In my experience, people don't change much."

"Please, Daed?"

Mr Eicher looked at his son. "You really do like her, don't you?" He scratched his head. "Alright, I will let you court her, for now. But I don't really see any future in it. I will give you two months to prove that she is worthy of you." He turned to go. "You should really think about courting a girl like Emma – they are the ones that make good wives, my son."

He walked away. Vernon stared after him for a while, then slowly turned back to the lathe.

Linda. She was so full of life, smiling and chatting. She was like a breath of fresh air. He had liked her for a while, but hadn't had the courage to approach her. He had enjoyed their date. But he had been unsure since – he knew that his father didn't approve of her.

He understood what his father meant about her. She did boast, and seemed unaware that she was doing it – or if she was aware, she didn't care. But she could change, couldn't she?

Vernon stared thoughtfully at the lathe.

He would have to have a talk with her about it, if he wanted to keep seeing her.

But how would she take it?

***

They laughed in the snow, throwing snowballs at each other, breathless.

Vernon stared at Linda as she ran, throwing snow behind her. Her face was aglow, and her dark hair was escaping her *kapps*. He didn't think he had ever seen a more vibrant girl. She really was like a light in the darkness.

Afterwards, over a hot chocolate at her kitchen table, they laughed.

He took her hand, lifting it to his mouth, and kissed it.

Linda gasped. Tremors ran through her, starting from the spot where Vernon had kissed her hand all the way to the soles of her feet.

He looked at her. The gaze seemed to go on forever.

"Linda." He stopped, as if he was unsure how to continue.

"*Ja?*" she breathed. She couldn't believe how blue his eyes were. They were the color of a cornflower, waving in the breeze on a hot summer's day.

"I like you, you know that." He looked uncomfortable. "I like you a lot. I want to keep courting you. But there is something that I need to talk to you about."

"What is it?" She picked up her hot chocolate and took a sip, surprised to see her hands were shaking slightly.

"It's the way you boast." He shifted in the chair. "Everyone says it about you. About how you boast about your singing."

Linda felt the hairs on the back of her neck start to bristle. "That is their opinion," she said. "Why should I let the small minds of other people effect the way that I feel about myself?"

She looked at him. "You don't care about such silliness, do you?"

Vernon sighed. "Like I said, I like you a lot," he said. "More and more every time we are together. But it does worry me. You were very loud and boastful when Mrs Albrecht complimented you after the Service last Sunday. People notice, and talk. I think you should just tone it down a little, that's all."

She felt her face reddening. "Do you think I have a lovely voice?"

"*Ja*, but..."

"But nothing." She stood up, gathering the cups. "It is known. I'm not making it up – I have been told forever how lovely my voice is. Why should I deny it, just because a few small minded people have a problem with how I talk?"

"But, Linda…"

"I think you should go, now." She turned away from him.

He sighed deeply, but picked up his hat and stood to leave.

"If that's how you feel," he said.

"That's how I feel."

He turned and walked toward the door. "Can I see you again?"

She looked at him, then softened. "Of course, Vernon. You know how much I like you."

"Shake my hand, then," he said, offering his own.

She walked toward him, putting her hand in his.

They both gasped at the electric current which sparked between them.

Vernon sat in the buggy to collect his thoughts before he left the Heiser's farm.

She wasn't interested in talking about it. She had bristled as soon as he had brought it up.

Which was a real problem.

He knew now that he loved her, and wanted her to be his wife.

But how could he convince his father?

***

Linda set the table for dinner that night, deep in thought.

Vernon. He was the sweetest, gentlest man she had ever met. Kind, polite, respectful…and his touch electrified her in a way that she had never dreamt possible. Was this love?

But what about what he had said to her? That she boasted too much? How could she think seriously about a man who thought that she was flippant and vain?

Linda knew that she was forward, and spoke her mind. She knew that the elders, especially, thought her not meek enough.

But she was who she was – how could she change that, for anyone?

Even if it was for Vernon.

"Let us pray." The family sat down for dinner, her father at the head of the table.

She dropped her head, as they prayed silently before their meal.

She usually rushed through it, eager to think of other things, or wolf down the meal in front of her.

But tonight, she closed her eyes and formulated her prayer.

Dear Lord, Thank you for the meal that we are about to eat. I am grateful for this bounty, and for my family sitting here, safe and well.

She frowned slightly, then thought more.

Thank you for Vernon, and the relationship that I feel developing between us. He is such a good man, Lord. I want to please him and be the best woman that I can for him.

But Lord, how do I stop being myself? If he wants me, shouldn't he accept the way that I am? How can I change for him? But most importantly, Lord – do you want me to?

She still had her eyes closed as the family slowly picked up their utensils and started eating.

"Linda?"

Her mother's soft voice roused her. She shook her head, then slowly picked up her knife and fork.

Mrs Heiser looked at her daughter. Linda was in an unusually pensive mood tonight. It wasn't like her rambunctious daughter to get lost in contemplation, especially at the dinner table.

What was happening with her? Whatever it was, Mrs Heiser thought it was transforming her – for the better.

***

Christmas had come and gone, and New Year was upon them.

Linda stared out the window, at the snow blanketing the terrain. She couldn't believe sometimes how much things had changed.

She and Vernon were officially an item.

He wasn't the type of man she had expected to find herself with.

He was solemn, and thought before he spoke. He was slow to smile and laugh, but when he did, his joy was fulsome. He was in every way the polar opposite of her – she, who was so quick to act, and left thinking to afterwards.

But she thought that they complemented each other well. She gave him energy when his flagged. And he gave her fresh perspective, a new approach to life. She admired his hard work and discipline – she was usually so flighty, she had to force herself to be still.

But there was one thing that troubled her.

He hadn't mentioned love or marriage, or even spoke as if they had a permanent future together.

She remembered the look on his face after the Christmas singing at the local nursing home.

He had joined her, although he usually didn't. Their choir numbered about ten, and was usually the same people from year to year.

The old people had sat in the lounge of the home, blankets over their laps, gazing expectantly. The group had rehearsed for a few weeks prior, and had their set list of favorites, such as *Silent Night* and *Away In A Manger.*

It had started well. Vernon had led the prayer prior, and then they had started singing, moving rapidly through their repertoire.

The old people had loved it, singing along with them and clapping their hands. She had noticed an old lady at the front, who whispered to one of the staff when their set was over. The nurse had approached her.

"Gladys wants to know if you could sing a carol by yourself. She said you have such a beautiful voice, she would love to hear you," the nurse had said.

Linda could see Vernon frowning, shaking his head no. But she couldn't disappoint an old lady, could she?

"I'd be delighted," she said.

She started singing *Angels We Have Heard On High*, one of her favorites that hadn't made the main list this year. She could hear the gasps of appreciation from the old people, and they clapped thunderingly when she finished.

She bowed, glowing with happiness. She felt like she was on cloud nine, as if her feet couldn't touch the ground.

But when she looked back at Vernon, his face was dark.

In the buggy on the way home that night, he didn't speak to her. They pulled up at her house, and she climbed down, waiting for him to say something.

"Vernon, are you angry with me?" Her voice was tremulous.

He gazed to the front, not looking at her. "I wonder that you want to make a spectacle of yourself."

She blanched. "The old lady asked me to sing!" She tried to swallow the lump that had formed in her throat. "It would have been discourteous to refuse."

"But why do you have to take such pleasure in it? Being the centre of attention, like a bird preening its feathers?"

She felt tears pricking behind her eyes. "You don't understand," she said. How could she explain it? "It comes through me. It is like a gift that I feel that I am giving to the world. It feels holy, like God commands it. Don't you have anything that you feel that way about? What about your wood work – you are so talented at it! Don't you feel that you would be denying the world something if you didn't work with your hands, making that beautiful furniture?"

He slowly looked at her. "I do like wood work," he whispered. "I do feel holy in its pursuit. *Ja,* I do understand what you mean when you say that."

She swallowed. "I am trying, Vernon," she said. "But it is hard. I am who I am. Why can't you accept me?"

He stared at her. "I am sorry to pain you, Linda. I know you are trying." He looked away. How could he explain his father's conditions? That she must show that she was becoming less vain about her voice?

She wouldn't understand. She thought that taking pride in her voice was as natural as breathing.

Vernon frowned. She was like a peacock, showy with her beautiful feathers. But the peacock had just as much right to exist as the less showy sparrow, didn't it? Just because one was different to the other, didn't make either of them wrong.

It was becoming too hard. "I will speak to you, soon." He picked up the reins, spurring the horses on into the night.

Linda had stared after him, until he was a pin prick in the distance.

She thought of it now, as she stared out the window. Would he ever learn to accept her, the way that she was? Or would he be forever trying to change her?

***

He asked to speak to her, alone, the very next night.

She couldn't help but feel a small flicker of excitement. Was this going to be it? Was he going to propose to her?

But she was ambivalent. The better part of her longed for him, would walk to the ends of the earth to be his wife. The worst part of her was resentful at his insistence that she change who she was. What would be her answer, if he did ask her?

He walked into the house, taking off his hat, stamping his feet on the door mat to get rid of snow clinging to his pants.

Her mother greeted him, then made a discreet exit. Linda thought that her mother probably thought that this was going to be a proposal, too.

They sat down at the kitchen table, after Linda had poured them both a coffee. He stared at his cup for a long, long time before he looked at her.

"Linda…" His voice trailed off. He swallowed awkwardly.

"*Ja*?" She smiled, tentatively.

"It's like this." He swallowed again. "My father has put a condition on me courting you. He says that you must change; show that you are not boasting anymore, before he will agree to me putting a proposal of marriage to you." He looked down at his coffee cup again.

"What?" Linda thought that she had misheard. Mr Eicher was dictating that she had to change?

Then it hit her, right in the solar plexus. It felt like she was back in the school yard, when Jebediah King had pushed her so hard she had hit the ground, winded.

"Linda, it is possible." He reached out for her hand, picking it up. She didn't resist. "You just have to tone it down a little. Pretend you are Emma Sommer."

"Pretend I am Emma Sommer?" she repeated, looking down at her hand in his.

"Well, I didn't mean that exactly, of course." He let her hand go, running his own through his hair. This wasn't going exactly as he wanted it to. "I mean, try to act like her a little – you know how meek she is, barely saying boo to anyone. Blushing when anyone says anything to her. Then my father might agree to us marrying."

"You want me to act like Emma Sommer?" she repeated. "So that your father will agree to us marrying?"

"*Ja*," he nodded. Did she understand him, after all? He looked at her, ready to smile.

But Linda wasn't smiling. In fact, he had rarely seen her so angry. She stood up.

"You can tell your father," she said, carefully, "that I have no intention of changing for anyone. And as far as us marrying goes – well, Vernon Eicher, I wouldn't marry you if you were the last man on earth!"

He paled. "What?" he stammered.

"You heard me," she continued. "The front of you! You haven't even asked *me*, Vernon, if I want to marry you, before you ask *your father*?" She shook her head. "You presume too much! I don't care to discuss it at all! I would like you to leave, now."

Vernon stood up. He was shaking. "Linda..."

"No," she said. She didn't look at him, picking up his hat and giving it to him. "Good bye, Vernon."

"Oh, and one more thing," she said. "You can tell your father that I wouldn't want to be Emma Sommer in my wildest dreams."

She pushed him out of the door, then leaned against it, breathing heavily.

The tears when they came were hot and salty. It felt good to release them.

***

Mrs Heiser looked at her daughter. This was the second day now that Linda had slept in, claiming that she was coming down with a cold.

She knew her daughter, knew that a mere cold couldn't shake that indomitable energy.

But something had. And she would bet that something had a name: Vernon Eicher.

"So what happened between you and Vernon?" she said, from the doorway.

Linda glanced at her mother, pulling the blankets higher. "Nothing."

Mrs Heiser sighed. "Linda, it's obvious. You have been in a black mood ever since he left on Tuesday night."

Linda sat up suddenly. "He wants me to be Emma Sommer!"

"What?" Mrs Heiser wasn't expecting that. "The Sommers from the next town's youngest girl? What on earth are you talking about?"

Linda laughed suddenly, a bit hysterically. "I am not good enough for his father, apparently. They both want me to act like Emma

Sommer, if not actually *be* her. Why doesn't Vernon just court her instead? Then he, his father and Emma can all ride off into the sunset together, happy as larks!"

"Linda," her mother scolded.

Linda's bottom lip trembled, and she burst into tears.

Her mother came toward her, putting her arms around her. "Hush, now," she said, crooning. "It will be all right. Take a deep breath and calm yourself."

Linda took a deep breath, but the tears kept coming. "He doesn't love me, Mamm. Not for who I am."

"What does he say?" her mother asked, gently.

"He says that I boast too much about my voice," she said. "His father thinks that I am full of pride, and wants me to change before he will give his stamp of approval to Vernon to ask for my hand in marriage."

Mrs Heiser sighed. "That is hard, Linda." She paused, looking at her daughter. "How does Vernon feel about that?"

"I don't know," Linda replied. "He has often said that he thinks me too boastful, but he hasn't mentioned his father before. He was mad at me for singing solo at the nursing home at Christmas. Said that I should have refused, that I was taking pride in being asked to sing by myself."

"Well," said Mrs Heiser, "that would be hard for Vernon – having his father put conditions on his courtship with you. Vernon must be torn. I have observed him with you, Linda, and he really does have a great respect for you."

Linda's eyes softened. "Do you think so? Why does he want to change me, then?"

"I don't think he is trying to change you, not really," her mother responded. "He has asked you to tone things down, not to boast. Is that so hard? Maybe he shouldn't have got mad at you for singing solo, not when you were asked specifically. It would have been rude to refuse

– and besides, it gave joy to those poor old people in that home at Christmas. He has confused it, a bit. But then he is under pressure from his father."

Linda nodded, slowly. "I think I understand, a little. At least, I understand how hard it must be for Vernon."

Her mother kissed her, standing up. "I want you to do something for me," she said. "I want you to study your bible tonight. Really study it. Try to see the truth in what Vernon asks you – for it is the truth, my *lieb*. You boast, and we have spoken about it many times. I want you to reflect on the difference between boasting and taking pride in a job well done."

Linda looked up at her mother, and nodded. "All right, Mamm. I will try."

"Good girl," her mother said, ruffling her hair. Then she left.

Linda stared down at her bible on the bedside table.

She would get up, do her chores, and she would study it tonight, just like her mother asked her to.

***

She sat down at her dressing table that night, lit her lantern and opened it up.

Her mother had directed her to some passages.

The first was Proverbs 27:2, which stated, "Let another praise you, and not your own mouth; a stranger, and not your own lips." She sat back and thought.

The quote was saying that people could praise you, but that you shouldn't praise yourself. It wasn't saying that your gift, or skill, or talent, couldn't exist in the world for other people to enjoy.

Perhaps that was what she had always been fearful of: that if she admitted that she boasted and that it was wrong, it would mean she mustn't share her gift with the world. That scared her. She felt she must sing like she must breathe. It was essential to her nature.

Then she read Psalms 10:4, which stated that people who are proud are so consumed with themselves that their thoughts weren't with God. That pride got in the way of real communion with Him.

She could see the truth in that. When she was boasting, her thoughts weren't with God; she was self-absorbed, basking in her own glory. She thought of the difference between her thrill at seeing the old people react with such joy at her singing, to her feeling of smugness when someone told her how lovely her voice was, or when she boasted about it. There was a world of difference: one was satisfaction at giving joy, the other was pride. Pure and simple.

Linda closed the book, deep in thought. She must talk to Vernon.

There were things they must discuss. She must try to bridge the gap that had sprung up between them.

***

He came around the next day, as she requested.

Her family were absent, had made themselves busy doing other things. She inwardly thanked them; it was essential that they had privacy.

He sat down at the table. She had made a fresh pot of coffee and a cinnamon coffee cake, which was still hot from the oven.

"Would you like a slice?" she asked. He nodded, in silence.

It was awkward, there was no doubt about that. She tried to smile, but it emerged a bit lopsided.

He picked up his fork, and took a bite. "It's good," he said.

She was about to say that of course it was, it was her grandmother's famous recipe, then she stopped herself. Her grandmother wouldn't have said that. Her grandmother would have nodded, remarked that she was glad he enjoyed it, and left it at that.

So that's exactly what Linda did.

It felt good; lighter, somehow. He picked up his coffee cup, and watched her.

"Vernon," she said. "I asked you here because I wanted to apologise."

His eyebrows raised. He wasn't used to Linda saying sorry for anything.

"I think I finally understand," she continued. "What you were saying, about being boastful. I have thought a lot about it." She stopped, looking at him. He nodded encouragement.

"I was scared," she admitted. "Scared that if I accepted what everyone told me, I wouldn't be able to sing anymore. That I was saying it was wrong to do so. But that's not what you mean, is it?"

"Of course not," he said. "I have never said you aren't able to sing."

"It felt that way, after the nursing home," she said, lowering her eyes.

He reddened. "It came out all wrong," he said. "I know it sounded like I was saying that you shouldn't have sung. But you were right, then. It gave such joy to the people it would have been wrong to deny them. I was just frustrated. I was under pressure from my father."

"I know," she said. "It must have been hard."

He looked at her. "Very hard," he said. He groped for his words. "I'm sorry about the other day. I don't want you to be Emma Sommer! I like you, Linda. In fact..." he paused, reddening. "I love you."

She gasped. "Oh, Vernon. I love you, too."

He stood up, overwhelmed. "I have been longing to tell you, for so long! But I didn't want to mention it, in case my father stood in our way."

"I know you are right, now," she said. "I will never boast again. I understand how it makes me appear to others, and how wrong it is to be so self-absorbed."

He looked at her, his eyes shining. "If I can speak to my father and get his approval, will you consent to be my wife?"

She flung her arms around him. "Oh, yes, Vernon. Yes, please!"

They kissed, tenderly.

"I am going, this minute," he said, grabbing his hat. "I have to speak to him." He kissed her, again, and then was off.

She stared at him through the window.

Vernon loved her. She loved Vernon. Hopefully, she would be his wife, soon.

If Mr Eicher would allow it.

***

Vernon came back later that day, with shining eyes.

"I spoke to my father," he said. "He is allowing it! I explained our conversations, and how you finally understand about pride. He is satisfied." He beamed at her.

"So we can be married?" she breathed.

"If you'll have me," he responded, suddenly shy.

"I would walk the ends of the earth to be your wife," she said, simply.

They embraced.

It was true – she loved him for eternity.

She was the luckiest woman in the world. And she would never boast again.